Romance ...
is that what makes us
fall in love?

Or, is it falling in love
that makes everything
romantic?

Come ... rediscover romance
and fall in love ...
with Ponder Romance.

Also from Ponder Romance

Sand Pirates

Ellis Hoff

A Ponder Romance

Published by Ponder Publishing Inc.

Sand Pirates

A Ponder Romance Book
Published by Ponder Publishing Inc.
P.O. Box 23037 RPO McGillivray
Winnipeg, Manitoba
R3T 5S3 Canada

U.S. Address: 60 East 42nd Street, Suite 1166, New York, New York, 101655
Internet address: http://www.ponderpublishing.com

Cover Photography (inset): Copyright D. Barton Used by permission.

Cover Design: PeR Design

ISBN 0-9681587-2-2

Printed in Canada

PROLOGUE

Lake Superior

"Oh," the woman sighs with relief, "clouds. Maybe we won't roast out here after all." A hand goes to her moist brow, the back of it pushing away damp, heavy hair.

"Another Zin?" her companion holds up the bottle a fleeting moment before filling his own glass.

"No, I'm okay. I think I will take a piece of —" She lunges towards him, nearly losing her footing, as if the boat's bottom has suddenly been pulled out from under her. Without meaning to, she catches the imitation-glass plate midair, but the Brie, slimy and fluid from the day's sun, slides off of it and stretches out in long, skinny fingers across the planked floor.

She twists towards the sky behind her. It is dark, ominous. "Shouldn't we head back?"

"Ah, well," he gropes for words that seem to come less easy than the nautical jive he's tossed around all day, "it's just a — a header from the north ... not to worry."

She looks at him. Hard. The *sailor*. The day's navigator. All day he's tried impressing her with his seafaring capabilities, his *heave ho!* and other jargon she is fairly certain he'd been making up as he went. A header from the north? Even she, limited severely when it comes to any kind of marine or meteoric wisdom, could have pulled out that one. They were on the lake. The big one. *The big lake they called Gitchigume* comes lyrically to mind via a Gordon Lightfoot flash-back. *Header* was just a silly way of saying headwind and those almost always came from the north.

She twists again, remembering that the Edmund Fitzgerald had literally disappeared in a matter of minutes during a storm on this very lake. She should have been watching. She'd nearly fallen asleep in the sun, lulled by the gentle rocking of the little boat and her need to escape his pretentious chit chat which was making this date, their first — and she was sure — their last, unbearable.

Suddenly it dawns on her, as the boat pitches and she watches the Zinfandel he is reaching for a shoot across the air and smash to the deck, spraying wine everywhere, that she might have to depend on him for her life.

"Are we supposed to get rain?" She means to ask this casually, but her words are edged in apprehension.

He smiles and says, "Nothing major," but his demeanor suffers a hairline crack. "But, you never can tell. If you're worried, we can go in."

"Please."

Too late.

Whitecaps. Then a sudden gust catches the mainsail and tips the boat so they both lose their footing.

"We have to go in," she says, getting to her feet, stumbling backwards and then trying again with slightly better luck, no longer worried about disguising her anxiety. "We have to turn around and get back now!" she yells even as he stumbles to the stern and attempts to work the riggings, the gust now a gale, the boat rocking violently.

"Get back here and steer!" he screams. "I can't do

everything."

On hands and knees, she thinks he can't do *anything*. She makes her way to the back of the boat, and when she gets there, it's all she can do to grab onto the handle. She uses every bit of power she can summon to inch the tiller to the right, and miraculously, the boat begins to turn, though still bobbing and pitching. The boat lurches forward, frothy tops of waves jumping over the bow.

Suddenly, it does not rock as violently as before; it is almost still, but there is an odd sensation, as if she is rising. She turns to the bow and discovers that it is under the water. Gravity jerks her forward, snapping her hands free of the handle and lurching her into the mainsail halfway down. She hangs on with her life until the back drops and the hull levels out.

Thunder cracks the sky open and she is pummeled with cold fists of rain. Above the deafening rage, she thinks she hears someone yelling, "Abandon ship!" She wrenches herself towards the sound. He is half-submerged, having abandoned the sail and desperately searching. "Life jackets!" he screams. "Where are they?"

She lets go and crouches into the swirling coldness, feeling all around. Her hands are cold, numb, but find the inside wall of the boat, grabbing things she cannot see but feel attached. A rod ... or handle ... a sharp, pointy thing ... a rope.

A rope!

Numb fingers pull it, hand over hand. It is the longest rope on earth, but it is a rope and will have an end. And maybe, just maybe ...

She knows what it is the moment she touches it. It pulls her up, which means the boat is going down. She pulls herself clumsily onto it, feeling, in the last split second, the floor of the boat separating from her feet.

"I found one!" she screams into the drenching

wind. "We'll have to share!" He does not answer and
she cannot see him. "I'm — I'm going to hold it out
so — so," her lips are trembling, her words frozen,
"you can grab onto it." She hopes he can hear. It
sounded plausible, even in her chilled stutter, but it
was insane. She doubted it could support the weight of
two people. The only crazier thing to do was nothing
at all.

She feels a tug.

The float is torn from her grasp, ripped away by
something stronger, more determined. Deliberate. She
is dumbstruck. Alone, freezing, and being smothered
by cold shifting mountains of water, she can do
nothing.

Crack!

The boat. What was left of it. Torn in different
directions and her, rising high above it on the crest of
a water swell, sees the wreckage, illuminated by light-
ning, before being tossed unmercifully, forcefully onto
it, the mainsail traveling towards her at the speed of
light.

***

He struggled across the rocky-bottomed shoreline,
jagged edges pushing into the soles of his feet with
every heavy, water-logged step. Gone were the expen-
sive canvas oxfords he'd borrowed, so to speak, from
an old roommate. Then he remembered the watch and
stopped dead in his tracks, dropping the life preserver
onto the shallow water with an unnerving *thwack*.

It was there. Hallelujah! There was order to the
universe after all. The Rolex, with its gold octagon
face, had become a logo, of sorts, for him, a good-luck
piece with extraordinary powers over discriminating
folk with more money than brains. Had he lost the

watch, he might have actually considered paddling back in search of it.

He proceeded, cursing the time and money he'd spent removing the callouses that once protected his now-ravaged feet. He staggered onto smoothened sand and collapsed.

"We're getting you help!" came a voice behind the man, so completely unexpected it startled him visibly. "Stay where you are!" it continued. The man, quite weary now, turned at the waist towards the sound. He waved unenthusiastically, letting the woman know he'd heard, then turned back. He was tired. Near death experiences were a drain. He heard sirens. They were barely audible but growing in intensity. For him, he thought. A whole fleet. Then he saw it. *Her*.

"Well, well, look who showed up at the party after all."

At least, he *thought* it was her. Either that or a sea monster. A tangled mess of bare, bluish limbs and stringy green weeds; a fleshy clump, face down in the shallow water, long red tendrils spilling out around her like blood.

It was her. The clincher was the wreckage some twenty feet out, bobbing a slow getaway. The blue green color of the hull had annoyed him from the start. Had it brought her out? he wondered. Had she been unconscious to the end?

The sirens were deafening now. The woman above was flapping her arms and saying something he could not hear and did not need to know. He looked at the dead woman ten feet away. An hour ago they'd shared a spendy bottle of White Zinfandel. He would have to touch her. He didn't want to, but he would have to. It would look funny if he didn't.

The skin on her upper arms was cool to the touch, as cold as it was blue, but when his fingers pressed into the fleshiness, there was a mushy, pulsing warmth ... was she alive?

His answer came in the form of a hideous sound, something between a gasp and a belch. He jumped back instinctively, and watched as she rose up on the arms he'd been fingering, water and greenery shooting out of her hair-fenced mouth, her body gyrating as she rolled onto her back.

Over his shoulder he saw the rescue crew working their way down the steep, sandy embankment. He moved towards the woman. Her eyes were closed, her breath shallow. There was, he knew, only one way to work this.

He crouched directly over her and closed his eyes. He had never given mouth-to-mouth, had only television re-enactments to rely on, but it didn't matter. She didn't need it. He cringed as his mouth made contact with the weed-spewing one. She tried, weakly, to squirm away, so he grabbed her face on both sides and delivered a second unnecessary breath. Suddenly her eyes flew open so wide he was reminded of female victims in low-budget movies.

"I'm saving your life," he barked defensively, then softened, brushing hair back from her eyes. "I'm saving your life." There! Small and weak, but he saw it. A smile. She didn't remember.

ONE

One Year Later...

Frans Vondel leaned against the battered red Datsun, occasionally shading his eyes against the hot Caribbean sun, and watched passengers climb the ramp to the cruise ship. This could not be happening. Not to him. Not after all the work. A five-year investigation and six months deep undercover on this island only to come up empty-handed. What could have possibly tipped Trumad off? Everything was so tight, so certain. They had him. He drummed his large fingers impatiently on the dusty car roof. They had no choice now but to intervene, once the ship was on its way, blowing their cover and severing all links to the elusive crime lord. There was no point hanging around any longer.

***

Petra Logan swallowed a mouthful of dirt as she rounded another sharp turn, the old car racing past scrubby vegetation and dusty dunes, forcing geckos, birds and insects to madly scramble out of the way as she tore along. The scenic route. Probably the only route, Petra thought as the rattling vehicle bounced around another bend. Another joke. She'd never been anywhere before where the main road was dirt. Not even dirt. Volcanic residue. That was the island of

Sava for you, in a nutshell.

Well, she wouldn't be here much longer. Mere minutes and she'd be off this oversized sand dune, this pit stop in the Carribean occupied by a gathering of mixed souls whose ancestry ranged wildly from Dutch, French and Chinese to self-proclaimed Caribbean, African and East Indian. There were so many dialects spoken among the small populace Petra wondered how they communicated amongst themselves let alone outsiders. You'd think that somewhere along the way they'd have at least developed some kind of common mode of communication.

She could see the stack of the cruise ship now and the aqua waters peeking through the vegetation at the end of Sava's main drag. Couldn't this old wreck go any faster? She had her foot to the floor. The pier came into view and she sighed audibly. "Ah, air conditioning!" The hotel supposedly had it; at least that's what the sign outside had said. Obviously on Sava that meant windows.

She slammed on the brakes as the car approached the pier, and barely taking the time to throw it in park and turn off the engine, tossed the keys on the dash and jumped out. Whoever Clark had rented it from would find it sooner or later; it'd be pretty hard to miss on an island only five-square-miles big.

"Madam, move away from the car and keep your hands in plain sight!"

Slamming the door, Petra jumped at the sharp command, and spun around to the source of the mild Dutch accent, the unbridled trade winds blowing long red curls straight across her face. Did this wind never stop? She shoved the long bands of hair back and flicked her head so that the wind caught the unruly tresses and blew them behind her.

"Away from the car, please."

Was he talking to her?

A formidable man with shaggy, sun-bleached hair and some sort of uniform she thought looked more like safari gear, was staring down at her with an unquestionable air of authority, his face impossible to find with the sun behind him practically blinding her. He beckoned her forward.

Had she been speeding? Well, yes, she had, but with good reason. "Look," she began coolly, but not budging, "I don't know what this is about, but I don't have time —" Was that the boarding plank pulling away? She shaded her eyes with a hand, and peered down the long shoreline to the front of the cruise ship. If she yelled *wait* would they hear her?

"Madam, may I see your identification."

"No!" She glanced from him to the boat, then back again. "I mean, I don't have it." Everything from her sunglasses to her toothbrush was on that boat, including her purse and identification. "Look, just give me the ticket and I'll pay it. I'll — I'll mail it to you."

She took two quick steps, but the man put himself in front of her, his wide back blocking the high-powered sun, and Petra no longer needed to shade her eyes to see his face. His eyes. Hard steel and blue. Demanding.

She tried to step around him, but he put out a tanned and powerful-looking arm.

"Identification?" he asked again.

She could see by the firm set of his wide jaw and the hard chisel of his cheek that he would not be moved. She backed away, shook the head of curls out of her eyes, and fleetingly considered trying to outrun him. A ghost of a smile appeared in his eyes as if reacting to that thought.

"I told you, it's on the boat." She couldn't help sizing up the distance from him to the dock.

"That is very unfortunate," he replied, his tone ominous. "Whose car is this?"

"I don't know. It's a rental. Does it matter? I have to catch that boat." Her glance dropped to his waist to check for a gun. There definitely was one. Was it loaded?

His eyes followed her glance. "Where did you rent it from?"

A loud horn sounded several short toots that Petra recognized as a parting pattern. "How would I know? I was only driving it. Now listen, that boat out there is waiting for me. Just give me the blasted ticket already. I don't have time for this!"

"You will need to make the time, Madam. There is a little problem with this car."

Petra swallowed air and looked nervously over the top of the rusty sedan to the distant ship. Was it her imagination or was it moving? Slowly? It wouldn't depart without her, would it? Surely Clark knew she wasn't on board yet. He hadn't really believed her when she'd told him she wasn't going, had he? No. That was impossible. All her things were on the ship, had been since early this morning.

"Then it's your little problem," Petra said hotly, trying to edge her way around him. "It's your little island, right? Do whatever it is you usually do but I've got to get down that dock; they're leaving!" He blocked her path again. "Please," Petra despised herself for begging, "this car, whatever's going on with it, doesn't involve me. I've got to make that boat."

"Then we both have a problem, madam."

"No!" she cried. "I can't miss —" It *was* moving. Water played about its huge bow with insignificant little turquoise ripples that seemed highly significant to her. It couldn't leave without her. *It couldn't*. Petra's breath stuck somewhere between her chest and her chin, the onset of tears stinging her eyes. This wasn't happening. She had never been so anxious to leave anywhere as she had Sava, with its dirty, thatched-roofed huts and rusty old cars, like the ancient white van with more rust than steel ambling across the lot. Why wasn't this guy bothering that driver? That vehicle, bucking and wheezing, was an obvious road hazard. Why was he picking on her?

She watched helplessly as the ship, now several hundred feet from the end of the pier, merrily sailed off, utterly oblivious to the fact that she hadn't so much as a dime on her, let alone a change of clothes. Didn't anyone notice or care that she wasn't aboard?

Petra turned to glare at the man who'd derailed her escape from vacation hell. "I want to speak with an attorney. Immediately! I will not discuss anything with you, and that includes answering your idiotic questions, until I have conferred with counsel." *There!* "Oh, and another thing: you deliberately kept me from boarding the *Surf Queen* and should make arrangements to undo this huge, oh, and I do mean huge, faux pas as soon as humanly possible. I'm either on the next boat out of Sava or your life becomes a nightmare. Do we understand each other?"

***

Her temper outstripped her hair as far as fire went. Her profile had labeled her *impulsive*. Impulsive? He held his smile. Petra Logan was a tropical storm. She was also a long shot. His only shot. "I understand you very well, Madam," he said cordially. "You are free to catch the next ship leaving Sava."

This unexpected cooperation surprised her. She straightened her shoulders and cocked her chin with just a trace of haughtiness. "Well, thank you. I assume, then, that you will you arrange for my luggage to meet me at the next stop?" He nodded. She pushed the mass of wavy red tresses away from her face and managed a small smile. "Should I wait out on the pier?"

"Yes, of course, Madam. Be my guest." A deep grin threatened to escape.

Her smile widened, though still condescending, and he watched her stride regally towards the wooden planks. She had terrific legs. Long. Tanned. Smooth ... starting somewhere under her short white denim skirt, a skirt that encased slender hips. The view from the front had been pretty good too. The tight blue top matched her eyes, although he hadn't been paying so much attention to them as he had the alluring valley that dipped into the neckline.

She stopped by a bundle of crates and, glancing briefly towards him as if to surmise whether he might object, seated herself atop and, with crossed legs, a sandaled-foot swinging impatiently, rested her chin in a hand supported by an elbow on her knee. She began to hum quietly, the wind wildly whipping her hair about.

"It could be a wait," he called out.

Her foot ceased to swing. "How *much* of a wait?"

He strolled towards her, bracing himself for the fireworks. "Oh, let's see. This is Sunday so ... six days."

"Six days!" She pounced from the crates, as defiant as her blowing hair. "*Six days?* Are you out of your mind? I can't stay here six days. Call someone! Get a boat out here!"

He gave her an official frown and began walking towards his own vehicle. "Madam, I'm afraid that's not possible."

"What do you mean: not possible?" she continued to screech, almost running beside him as she followed him off the pier. "Of course it's possible. I'll call someone. A ... a charter service. A helicopter.

Whatever. Whatever it takes. I'm not staying on this two-bit sandbox for another six hours, let alone six days."

"A sand barge docks here every Thursday. If we have matters cleared up by then, perhaps the captain will let you hitch a ride," Frans told her amiably, stopping in front of his beat-up old Datsun. "But I feel it only fair to caution you that he is known to be somewhat of a ... how do you say it in America ... a lecher?"

Tears sprang to her blue eyes, the bluest eyes he'd ever seen.

"I can't ride on a barge! I can't wait either! Call someone and have them intercept the *Surf Queen*. My passport and credit cards are on board. I'm sure my f-fian ... uh ... companion will be helpful in locating them. They can be flown out to me. I don't care what it costs, just do it."

He made his smile appear accommodating. "Merchants here are the same as anywhere. They take payment up front, especially from tourists. And as I keep having to remind you, there are matters to be cleared up first."

"Matters! What matters?" her voice rose in pitch. "I've already told you I won't speak to you about anything until I've had the benefit of counsel. Call my lawyer."

Frans opened the Datsun's passenger door and gestured politely for her to be seated. "How am I going to do that? I don't even know your name."

TWO

Unbelievable! Clark Martin put the binoculars down and pulled himself away from the ship's railing as the last of Sava disappeared. Who else could screw up getting off an island?

And after all the trouble he went through to ensure she made it on! Maybe he should have intervened, but who knew why that stupid island cop had stopped her; some trumped-up driving infraction, likely. These island cops were always looking for a few extra bucks, but he wasn't about to draw attention to himself. What point would there be in both of them being stuck on the island? Knowing Petra, she'd have them both on the Savan chain gang in no time.

Now it was her problem ... hers and Trumad's.

***

"Please get in the car, Miss Doe."

"That's *Ms*. Doe to you."

"*Ms*. Doe, will you please get in the car."

He could say please until his face turned blue. "No, I don't think I will."

"Ms. Doe ..."

"What? What are you going to do? Overpower me?" she scoffed, tossing a mass of red tresses over her shoulder. "Handcuff me?" she added, turning her face back to his, words catching in her throat at the glint of steel at his waist.

In an instant, he caught her hand in his, snapping on the bracelet with a solid click. She stood there, her mouth hanging open, speechless and blinking impotently, scarcely conscious of the second click.

He smiled coyly, white teeth accentuated by his Savan tan. "Ms. Doe, get in the car. And please don't struggle. They tighten if you do."

***

Petra surveyed the brute driving the old Datsun. Scruffy. Shaggy. Muscles bulging everywhere. Sun-bleached hair waving every which way and in varied lengths displaying every shade of blond, like it couldn't make up its mind. Like his eyes. Were they grey or were they blue? And that blue ... not bright ... *unbending*. She supposed he might be considered handsome, maybe very handsome, that is, if you liked the rugged, masculine type. She knew women who did.

And he was tall. Really tall. And broad. After crawling into this ... *Savan* Cadillac, as best she could with these sadistic shackles, she had watched in a twisted sort of fascination as he neatly, automatically, folded his tall frame nearly in two and forced it into a space she would have sworn a moment before would never accommodate him.

"So, Ms. Doe," he said, breaking into her stony silence, "your identification is with your man?"

"Companion," Petra corrected bristly. Clark Martin hardly belonged to her anymore.

"Oh, yes, excuse me — your *companion* — he is not your husband?"

"Is that really any of your business?" She wasn't answering any more of his questions. The Datsun swung to the left, treating her, inconceivable as it was, to an even more primitive passage and a number of shabby buildings scattered along it, in no apparent order. "Where are you taking me?" she barked. "Headquarters?"

His eyes left the road and he chuckled, turning towards her. What was so funny? Was he planning on making a joke of her situation, her abandonment, to the other officers? Oh, just let him try. She was in no mood to be the entertainment of the Savan police force.

The rumbling vehicle came to a halt in front of a crumbling brick building void of distinguishing marks or any kind of sign or emblem. *Headquarters*, she supposed. Only on Sava.

Still, there had to be at least one rational cop who might understand her plight. And she was going to get to him. *First*. Clumsily, she yanked on the door handle. "Ouch!" she yelped, as cold steel cut into her wrists.

"Ms. Doe, I will be happy to assist you if you will be patient," he said, as he cut the engine.

"Happy to assist me to a cell, you mean," she spewed, instantly regretting her words; she'd already given him enough ideas. "How convenient that this handle doesn't work."

"Well, it is the closest thing to a police car on Sava. I can't have criminals running out on me every time I slow down or stop."

"Criminal?" she spouted. "I'm not a —" She broke off as he opened his door and began to climb out. "Where are you going?" she demanded, craning her head to peer at him through the rear window. "If you think for one minute you're leaving me out here while you go in there and tell all kinds of lies about me, you'd better think again." She banged on the door with her shoulder, wincing as the cuffs tightened yet again.

***

With a weighted sigh, Frans twisted her handle and waited silently for her to stop struggling before he tugged it open. Picking up a porcupine barehanded would be easier than keeping this blazing beauty under control. As he reached in, long bronzed legs kicked out, one at a time.

"I don't need your help, thank you," she huffed.

Frans stepped back. She'd only hurt herself by struggling against him; he'd wait until she calmed down. With effort, he averted his eyes, biting back a smile as she tried to extricate herself from the car while attempting to maintain the length of her incredibly short skirt.

Her sudden launch forward seemed to surprise even herself and she staggered on her feet. Frans lunged to catch her, but she twisted stubbornly out of reach, and fell into the sand with a sharp cry as the cuffs broke her fall. She gasped, as if trying to suck back the breath that had been knocked from her, then attempted to rise up on her elbows, wincing as she slumped back down, deflated.

Crouching, he slid his hands under her elbows and pulled them forward so that they could support her. He reached for her tiny hands. "I wish you hadn't struggled," he murmured, carefully unlocking the cuffs. He hadn't wanted to use them, but what else could he have done? Tears slid down her cheeks, dampening the sandy red locks hanging limply in front of her lowered face. Red welts circled her wrists. Gently, he brushed over them with his thumbs. "We'll fix this inside," he said, surprised by his own tenderness.

Vivid, faltering blue eyes rose to his, and for the

briefest instant a frightened, helpless and wounded woman returned his gaze. And for the first time in his life, Frans Vondel hated his job.

***

Folded into him. Held. Touched. All of her, bound to him, by his eyes. What would his real touch be like?

He *was* touching her. Her hands. She gazed down to find them cradled in his. Huge and strong, like the rest of him. Stroking her raw skin. Tenderly ... gently.

Her eyes travelled back up, lingering at his mouth. Full and wide. A hint of a grin turning up the corners, playing.

A grin? Playing? Was he playing with her? How dare he? She tossed his hands aside, scrambling to her feet. "You think this is amusing?" He rose from the sand, his huge shadow swallowing her up, pulling her closer, her senses stirred by the scent of musk and sea. She could feel it in her hair. On her skin. She couldn't breathe.

A slow smile spread across his face. A dangerous, reckless smile. Steel eyes hinted at something she couldn't comprehend. "Amusing is not the word I'd have chosen."

She choked out a breath, feeling sanity return with new air. She grasped at it blindly and held out her wrists to display the welts. "I'm sure my lawyer will find an appropriate term!"

Shaking the sand from her tangled tresses to conceal her trembling, she skirted around him and stalked to the building, flinging the door open.

It was dark. Too dark for an office in the daytime. And quiet. Musty.

Where were the desks, the warm bodies with badges? Maybe this wasn't headquarters after all. Then she saw it in the farthest corner. A cell. Bars. She'd never seen one before but there was no mistaking it. The room was suddenly flooded with light.

Petra swung around. "Where is everyone?" she demanded.

He tossed the keys onto the mess of papers on the lone desk. "This is it."

"This is it?" She scanned the room in distaste. "This is headquarters?"

"Actually, headquarters was your word." He said, settling down into the cracked leather chair that seemed to mold around his solid frame.

"I do get a phone call, don't I?" she inquired flippantly.

He gestured with one large shoulder to the black rotary on the desk. "Please."

Petra tromped to the desk and gripped the receiver. Her hand paused in mid air. This wasn't Minneapolis where she'd dial 911. Besides she was *at* 911, wasn't she? What about *zero*? Wasn't that the universal call for assistance? When you're off the charts, who did you call? Dialing, she avoided looking at the man. There had to be someone on this island who could push him around.

There was an ungodly long pause, then static and clicks filled the air between Petra and outside life forms. Then, a booming male voice speaking rapidly in what she supposed was Dutch or German. It didn't much matter. She was well acquainted with the currency of both sovereigns but, unfortunately, could not speak either language. A word here, a word there; it sounded like chit chat.

"Hello! Hello!" Petra shouted desperately into the receiver. "Do you speak English?" The quick-paced, foreign reply convinced her that he did not.

"En-glish?" Petra looked in frustration towards the

man who, under the guise of paperwork, was listening. Intently, she was sure as that smile played with the corners of his mouth again. He was enjoying this. She bit her lip and turned her back on him, more determined than ever to get through. "Hablo Espanole?" she pleaded direly. At this the blond man openly laughed.

"Burgomaster —"

"Burgomaster?" she repeated the word, which had some familiarity, into the receiver. She wasn't sure what it meant, exactly, but she was almost certain it had something to do with the government. A chief officer or an executive of the state or — or something. A big shot. Her heart began to pound. "Yes, yes! Burgomaster. I must speak to the Burgomaster!"

Hearty laughter filled the crackly line and Petra held the receiver in front of her and just stared at it. Then she looked at her captor, aghast. What was she supposed to do now?

The man stood up, seeming to fill the room with his large frame, and came to her from behind the desk. He took the receiver and covered the mouthpiece with his hand. "You want to speak with the Burgomaster?"

She handed over the phone and her fate. "Please," she said softly. What alternative did she have?

The man smiled, held her eyes a moment longer, then removed his hand from the receiver and began speaking rapidly, using the language of the other man. He laughed, spoke a bit more, then hung up and returned to the desk.

"I — I thought you were going to get the Burgomaster on the phone for me!" *What had she been thinking?*

"That won't be necessary," he said nonchalantly, going back to shuffling well-worn papers.

"Won't be —" Petra gulped air. "Won't be

necessary! What do you mean it won't be necessary?" Petra reached for the papers he pretended to be concentrating on and jerked them from his hands. His blue eyes met hers. Now she had his undivided attention.

"I demand to speak to the Burgomeister —"

"Burgomaster," he corrected.

"Whatever. I want to talk to the head honcho and I want to talk to him now. Get me the Burgomaster immediately. I mean it." She did. Oh, did she ever.

Wordlessly, and with unnerving calm, the man reached into the top drawer of the big metal desk and pulled out a wooden plaque. He placed it on edge nearest Petra so that the brass nameplate was visible to her.

Petra could feel the angry red blush on her face. "Oh, no, you're not —"

He smiled widely, leaned across the desk, balancing his long upper body on strong arms. "Burgomaster Frans Vondel, at your service, Madam."

***

He watched her mouth open, then close, then open again.

Frans gave her his most disarming smile. "I believe, until we get this matter straightened out, I will be your host here on Sava."

"Host?" Her bright blue eyes exploded with her voice. "I don't need a host! I need a lawyer! I'm only here because you chained me to this wretched island."

"Perhaps *host* was not quite correct, Ms. Doe," he continued, giving his smile some authority. "My duties on Sava include upholding the law, which you have clearly broken."

"Is that so? Well, I have rights too. Surely there is someone else on this island I can appeal to."

"Yes, of course. We are quite civilized on Sava despite the deceptiveness of our isolation and size," Frans replied amicably. "You may make an application to the judge."

She crossed her arms and tilted a mass of red tresses at him. "Well then, I insist on making an application."

Frans fiddled with papers on his desk and picked up a pen. "Hmm..."

She made a low growl. "And just precisely when does this judge come around?"

He kept his eyes engrossed in papers to prevent a grin. "It's usually every three months, so it's fortunate you will have to wait only one. But of course, if you prefer to deal with me, I can have this matter cleared up in a few days." He dropped the papers and added playfully, letting her see the grin, "I am a very experienced Burgomaster."

"No doubt!" she hissed. "Kindly tell me, Burgomaster Frondel —"

"*Vondel*," he corrected politely. "Frans Vondel."

"Yes, well," she looked away for just a second, as if his interruption, his easy manner, had unnerved her, "if you plan on keeping me here it is well within my rights to know what I'm being charged with."

"I haven't charged you with anything, Miss Doe."

"You can't keep me here without charging me with something."

"You want me to charge you with something?"

"No, of course I don't want you to charge me, but ... but you can't keep me from leaving here unless you do."

"Are you sure of that?" Frans asked in feigned seriousness, pulling out his chair and picking up a handbook on ham radio operations written in Dutch. "I could have sworn there was something in here about detainment with probable suspicion. Let me see," he said, seating himself and thumbing through the catalog.

"I don't believe this!"

"Oh, yes, here it is. Hm-m-m," he put his finger on a random article and nodded as if he were giving it deep consideration. "Just as I suspected."

She leaned across his desk. "*Please* enlighten me, Burgomaster."

Frans studied the page a moment longer, then lifted his head, his eyes hovering over a perfect feminine contour framed by wavy strands of fire. With effort he resumed a stern facade. "The auto you were operating was reported stolen."

She backed away. "*What?*"

"Operating a stolen vehicle is a crime. I think this is true also in America."

"I know it's a crime but I didn't steal it!"

"The fact that you were operating it is suspicious, would you not agree, Miss Doe?"

"Of course I agree but ..." She began to pace, moving fluidly, her body hypnotic, even in a rage. "I mean, no. I mean, well, I'm not a suspicious person and I'm not a car thief. I don't understand —"

"*Exactly!*" Frans slammed the little catalog shut and stood up, pushing the chair under his desk.

"Exactly what?"

"Well, you're the one operating a stolen auto and you don't understand, how am I, a simple island Burgomaster, supposed to make heads or tails of such suspicious activity? I have no choice but to investigate this matter."

"My — my traveling companion, Mr. Martin, was using that car during our stay."

"So, you are telling me this companion of yours, this Mr. Martin, stole the auto?"

"Yes ... I mean no."

"Yes or no, Miss Logan?" He could have bitten off his tongue. He'd used her name, but she didn't seem to notice.

"Well, Clark ... I mean, Mr. Martin, used the car during our stay but I was under the impression it was a rental. Mr. Martin is not the kind of man who would travel halfway around the world to steal a twenty-year-old Buick on a two-bit island."

"Chevy."

"Excuse me?"

"It's a Chevy. A nineteen-seventy-six Impala. Two tones, two doors, V-8 —"

"This is ridiculous!" Rage seized her again, igniting her features with passion and obliterating all else from his mind.

"What kind is he?" he asked.

"What *kind* is who?"

"Mr. Martin. Your traveling companion. He's not a car thief, or so you say. Tell me, Ms. Doe, what kind of man is he?"

Crossing her arms with a cold stare, she answered with a question of her own. "Tell me first, Burgomaster, what kind of man are you?"

Frans hesitated before answering. He hated having to hurt her, but someone had to open her eyes. "Hardly the type to leave my woman ... pardon me, my companion ... stranded in the middle of the ocean with nothing but the clothes on her back."

Her shoulders fell. Her voice dropped. "He didn't know I was going to miss the boat."

"He had no idea?"

"Well, no. Not really ... I mean, well, we'd gotten into this ... this ..." She eyed him suspiciously as if wondering how much she should confide in him. "disagreement and I threatened to stay behind."

"You told him you were not getting on the boat?"

"Well, yes, but ..."

"And your things? How is it they got on without you?"

"I guess Clark, I mean, Mr. Martin, just assumed I'd change my mind. *I had changed my mind*," she repeated firmly. "I was on my way when you — you arrested me!"

Frans played her own words back. "Was it this urgency, this *change of mind*, that compelled you to steal the auto?"

"Yes! I mean, no! I was in a hurry to get to the boat but I had no idea the car was stolen."

"Do you realize, Miss Doe, the penalty for being in a foreign country without a passport can be prison? You may not be willing to accept the blame for your circumstances, Madam, but rest assured they must be considered and investigated. This will take some time to be done properly."

He moved from his desk and played with the cluster of keys clipped to the belt-loop on his jeans, a subdued but portentous jangling wafting through the room.

The prettiest, and perhaps the angriest, eyes he'd ever seen narrowed at him. Hands jammed onto a small waist. "You think you're going to lock me up? I'm an American citizen! You can't lock me up!"

"I'd prefer to think of it more as you being my guest."

"Oh! You just wait! You don't know who you're dealing with!"

"That's the precisely the problem," he said, coming full circle.

She pivoted sharply. "Well, it's your problem Mr. Frondel! You just try keeping me here!"

Red hair flying behind her like a war flag, he watched her mad strut take her out the door. He knew he should go after her, and would, but perhaps a good stomp would calm her down.

Frans pushed the hair back from his brow with a smile. Perhaps, but not likely. He sighed heavily. The silence that followed in her wake was delicious.

Two days ago, from an obscure vantage point, Frans had monitored the arrival of Clark Martin, and his fiancée, Petra Logan. He'd recognized Martin immediately. Designer shirt, Italian shoes, Hollywood hair. He may as well have worn a sign around his neck: *Clark Martin — small time thug, big time moron.* So predictable, Frans hadn't wasted his breath laughing.

A good thing. He'd needed it. The case photos of Petra Logan provided an overall physical description but offered no hint of the unusual, fiery beauty that could not be captured on something so flat, so lifeless, as paper. He'd watched her get her land legs on the long pier as the ocean breeze lifted a curtain of wavy red tresses from her shoulders. She was tall, almost as tall as Martin, and dressed in a loose, flowing sort of dress that, working with the sea breeze, displayed a curvaceous, memorable figure. She'd turned at one point, towards him, completely unaware, and shaded her eyes.

He hadn't been able to look away, committing the shape of her mouth, the play of her features, to memory. Hardly the pathetic little creature he'd expected. The only child of Marshall Logan, founder of MidWest State Banks; an heiress who'd had to buy herself a man, even a silly excuse for one like Martin. It didn't make sense to him then, or now, that of all the men she could have, she'd ended up with Martin.

Frans rubbed a hand over his face, bringing logic back into his thoughts. He had a notorious criminal to catch and an island to run in the meantime. He was an Interpol operative, not a psychiatrist. If she was stuck on Martin, if a slick, self-serving jerk like that was what she wanted, why should he care?

On the other hand, say this slick, self-serving jerk was up to his neck in international money laundering and planning her murder, that would be another story. He was obliged to get involved. How deeply was a judgment call.

THREE

"I just feel so bad about Petra up and leaving you the way she did," the Barbie-doll-come-to-life crooned as she slicked oil over Clark's bare back. "Some people just don't appreciate what they have."

Clark smiled to himself and stretched out long and flat on the deck chair, reveling in the delicate touch of the shapely blonde, Mary Ellen Larkin. The street-smart young wife of the aging Texas millionaire who'd chosen this particular cruise because it was small, intimate and (Clark surmised after talking to Lenny at some length after one too many cocktails) void of the usual crowd of young men who were bold enough to ask his gorgeous young wife why she was with a man nearly three times her age. Clark had showered the rich Texan with subtle sympathies, all the while knowing he was one of those young men and that, at some point during the trip, he'd be alone with Lenny's wife, having just that conversation.

He'd been careful to appear understanding rather than judgmental. He was experienced at telling women things they wanted to hear and, more often than not, taking advantage of their vulnerable side once he had their undivided attention. With Mary Ellen it was a piece of cake. He'd been working on her since the *Surf Queen* set sail from Florida; a look here, a word there, innocent touches; it was all paying off now. He didn't need her money (something new) but her money made her more attractive. Clark liked the look of rich women. Clothes and hair were always a tip-off to the trained eye. Noses and bodies too. When this was over, he was going to find his own Mary Ellen.

But for now he'd make do with Lenny's. The old man couldn't begin to appreciate what he had, Clark mused while the buxom blonde nearly falling out of her hot pink bikini softly clawed well-manicured nails down to his waist. But Clark understood her perfectly. Understood and appreciated. A pretty face, a hot body and a mind like a calculator. Lenny had to be pushing seventy. He smoked like a chimney, ate like a lumberjack and drank like a fish. Clark gave him a year. Two tops.

The soft claws slid to the elastic of his waistband. He smiled and rolled onto his back. He was starting to feel like his old self again.

***

Anything for a glass of water.

Petra refused to stop walking. To stop moving away from her blond tormentor and whatever game he was playing.

Her pace had slowed significantly since she'd stormed out of the station. *Headquarters.* Her word. The nerve. The unbelievable gall. Who did he think he was? Well, the Burgomaster, of course, but really.

What kind of man is he?

He combs his hair with his fingers. That's what kind. Vondel. She saw him. Checking himself in the rearview mirror when he thought she wasn't looking. Sava's idea of primping. Clark had come prepared for the tropics with no less than a pick, a comb and three different kinds of spray he'd asked her to carry in her purse.

What kind is he?

What kind of a question was that?

The kind she should be able to answer. Clark Martin was, as in past tense, her fiancé and up until last night, she'd fully expected to marry him. She wasn't about to spill the intimate details of their relationship to the Burgomaster. Besides, there weren't any.

That was the problem.

Her problem.

It was the boating accident, of course. Lake Superior. She knew it. Clark knew it. Why could she never recall their passion that Clark had described in great detail, her insatiable hunger matched only by his stamina and expertise, an unquenchable fire ignited on their first date?

She'd tried a hundred times and a hundred different ways to breathe fire back into a relationship that should still be hot and heavy instead of cold.

Frigid.

Like the water that day. The frigid darkness he'd pulled her body from, never realizing her heart and passion had already sunk to depths he could not retrieve. If she'd managed to stay clear of the sail, if she'd seen the protective fight he must have put up to save her, at the risk of his own life, perhaps things would be different. But waking in Clark's arms, washed up on shore, had left her with some sort of intimacy phobia, which her therapist, at two hundred dollars a crack, had insisted she would get over in time. *If* she could only learn to trust Clark. Let go of the blame her therapist insisted she was hanging onto.

Poor Clark. The overwhelming, inexplicable revulsion that came over her every time he touched her, tried to get close to her, was oddly present, even now. He was so patient.

Frigid.

She hated the term, but it was accurate. He'd spent

the better part of a year doting on her, trying to coax her into his arms, into his bed. Little good it did either of them. Another man wouldn't put up with it or understand the way Clark did. Had.

Until last night.

Not even a romantic night on a Caribbean island, the expected highlight of what was supposed to be their elopement cruise, could douse her phobia. She'd come prepared to consummate their relationship with enough lingerie to put on her own trunk show. The green silk teddy with matching thong and kimono had seemed a sure bet. And was.

For Clark.

He'd come at her with a hunger that surpassed anything she'd fought off before. Maybe it was his aggressiveness, his eager hands and searching mouth, that made her snap. Too much, too fast — following a year of nothing.

She'd pushed him away. Again. Even though she'd promised she wouldn't, convinced herself that if she just forced herself, she'd overcome it.

This time it got ugly. He said things. Angry, hurtful things. The same things she'd said to herself a thousand times in the last year (though not quite the same words and not at the top of her lungs) and she'd said things back. One of them she remembered with deafening clarity: "Don't you ever come near me again."

Would he? Come near her again?

Oh, he had to. He just had to. She couldn't stay on Sava another six days. If it was over, it was over, but he wouldn't leave her behind, stranded, would he?

What kind is he?

Petra hoped with all her heart he was the kind of man who'd turn around at the next port of call and come back for her.

Before she died of dehydration.

***

"Mr. Martin." The young man looked embarrassed to have interrupted what looked like a highly-charged situation between two well-oiled sunbathing passengers. "There's a call for you."

Clark untangled himself from Mary Ellen, the hot skin pulling away with a slight, sticky tug where the oil had worn off. He grabbed a towel and threw it over her as they separated. He wasn't sure how much the steward had seen. He handed the bashful young man a twenty and pulled on his blue silk shirt with one hand while reaching for the portable receiver with the other.

"I'll see you at dinner?" Clark asked the stunned beauty, his hand over the mouthpiece.

"Uh, yeah. Sure."

Clark picked up the disappointment in her voice. She'd wanted him. Bad. They'd been so close. Now he was dismissing. Well, he thought smugly, she'd want him that much more next time. The pretty little gold digger who'd managed to wrap a Texas oil monger around her little finger with a flick of her blonde head and the deliberate motion of fine, slim hips was eating out of Clark's hand. He'd managed to get her top off in less than five minutes, all the while with her believing she was consoling him. Well, she was, but for things that had nothing to do with Petra Logan.

It would be her, Petra, on the phone, and he stalled, waiting for Mary Ellen to put her bikini top back on and exit the deck. She was moving in slow motion, taking every opportunity to stretch the task and curvy torso.

Damn! Petra wasn't even here and she was doing it. Ruining any chance he had for excitement or pleasure. She was going to be livid. Clark grimaced as he uncovered the mouth piece and spoke into it. "Clark

Martin."

"Is there something I should know?" a deep, male voice asked.

Trumad.

"I — I was just about to call you," Clark managed clumsily.

"Really?" Was Trumad's Dutch accent heavier than usual? "We had an agreement, and your end is sadly lacking. It was quite simple. Is there some way you know of drowning a woman by throwing her off a boat she is not on? You have some kind of magical powers? Perhaps you should be running this organization."

His accent *was* heavier. Clark could feel the blood pumping in his temples. "I will make it up to you."

"You will make it up to her." His cool, even tone, chilled Clark's blood.

Mary Ellen's bikini top came snapping against his head like a rubber band. "Is that Petra?"

"Not now!" Clark hissed, flinging the bikini top to the deck.

"Oh, yes, of course. How inconsiderate of me," Trumad sneered through the phone. "When would be convenient for you?" There was a silence. A long, menacing silence that threatened to come out of the receiver and strangle him.

"Uh, now?" Clark ventured.

"Good choice. Go back to Sava. Make up with her. Let the whole island know that you are a happy couple once again and wait for instructions." Trumad paused. "Do you need to write this down?"

"Don't worry about it."

"Don't make me."

"I'll arrange a boat right away."

"What?" screeched Mary Ellen. "You're going back to her?"

Clark couldn't think with her yapping and turned

away. "I hope this won't affect our relationship?"

"Oh, no, Mr. Martin," Trumad's voice was almost warm. "My plans for you haven't changed at all."

***

Frans glanced at his watch. She should have cooled off a little by now, although the way she'd torn out of here, she was probably halfway to town, cursing him with every breath and kicking up enough dust to scare away anyone who came near her. He'd better go get her before she hurt herself.

***

Lemonade. Iced Tea. A melting cherry Popsicle.
How could he have left her here?

Clark. The perfect man. Everyone said so. Everyone knew it. *She* knew it.

There was the other side, of course. He was a bit, well, full of himself. Pompous. Ostentatious. A little too quick to acknowledge pretty women, and a little too familiar with them once they noticed him. And, well, more than a little enamored with money. But Clark never made a secret of the way he felt about it. Besides, the daughter of one of the most successful bankers in America wasn't likely to end up with someone who didn't care about money, was she?

Her poor father. Clark was like a son. How was she going to tell him about their breakup? He worried so. And with good reason. He'd weathered bullfighters, bartenders ... oh, and there was that *thing* with the bowler.

That's why, when he'd finally put his foot down and insisted she come back to Minneapolis, work at his bank and learn the family business, she'd tried so hard to please him, tried to learn as much as she could. She felt like she was always disappointing him.

Petra had to admit that she wanted to settle down too. That's why she'd agreed to marry Clark. At thirty-two, she'd seen the world and more universities than she could recite offhand. Nothing stuck. Nothing ever seemed ... quite right. She couldn't keep up the impractical pursuit of *finding herself* forever. It was wearing thin and so was her father's patience.

Daddy wanted her to settle down with someone suitable. Someone safe. Have a family. He was backing Clark Martin for the job and she couldn't bear disappointing him. Again.

Petra smacked her dry, dusty lips.

Oh, for an ice cold beer. None of that imported stuff that Clark always insisted on, but a real beer, in one of those big frosty mugs with little shards of ice floating on top.

Then she heard it. Behind her. A vehicle. She turned. A van and *not* a red Datsun. Maybe now she could get out of the sun; maybe now she could finally get something to drink.

***

Frans raised his arms above the open doorway, using the metal frame to stretch deeply into the heavy Caribbean sun. Petra was nowhere in sight.

"Goin' somewhere, Frans?" a wiry boy of ten asked, stopping his bicycle. "She walk fast."

"She talk fast, too, Eric," Frans laughed.

"Maybe she got ride by now. In van."

Van? Frans arms dropped to his side. "What color van, Eric?"

"Maybe white, maybe rust."

***

Petra tried to ignore the men in the van. Her polite *Thank-you-for-taking-the-time-to-check-on-me-but-I-am-fine* had failed miserably. They had slowed to her pace, something between a crawl and an amble, making it obvious that they were not going to leave her alone.

She tried not to show fear, but these men were *huge*. They were sitting, of course, but this did nothing to diminish their obvious girth. Necks as big around as watermelons, shoulders like Toyota bumpers.

Maybe she could make a run for it.

Maybe? And her other choices were?

***

Roaring forward one breath ahead of its dusty wake, the Datsun rounded the corner.

There she was. Dangling from the side of the white van, struggling against thick arms trying to pull her in. The van picked up speed. Cursing, Frans rammed the gas pedal to the floor, a futile attempt to squeeze more speed from the rattling relic.

***

Petra's throat was too dry to scream. The kicking and twisting did nothing to loosen the paddle-thick fingers that dug mercilessly into her forearms, suspending her over the ground speeding beneath her feet in a brown-grey blur.

Another blur. *Red*.

Contemptuous grunts. "Burgomaster!"

The fingers released. The ground and sky were spun together. Her body banged over rocks and sticks.

Was someone calling her ... saying her name?

FOUR

Using a shoulder to push open the door, Frans
cradled her soft form into his chest, painfully aware of
how her languid body settled into the contours of his
own. Her head, softened by a pillow of red curls, lolled
into the crook of his neck, her warm breath both
reassuring and sensuous. The silence from her full,
perfectly-cut mouth, which had challenged her eyes for
attention from the first glance she'd thrown his way,
filled him with remorse. This was his doing. He willed
the fire back into her. To hear her words, even the
cutting ones, would be welcome. And those eyes, to
see them light up again.

He stepped over the threshold, carrying her like a
child ... no, like a bride. Her eyes opened. Blue.
Burning. He whispered, "*Petra.*" They closed, taking
the warmth with them.

***

"It just seems so —"

Mary Ellen appeared to struggle for words to
manage Clark's departure.

Leonard, the rich, old — and when it came to his
wife, hardly naive — Texan was in favor of Clark's
rerouting and had shown his support by making it
possible. A battered charter boat waited for Clark
down the pier in Caracas, equipped with a surly
looking crew. Clark wondered if the shape of the boat

and crew had anything to do with what he'd wanted, and almost gotten, from Lenny's wife.

"Damn romantic, if you ask me," Lenny jumped in with his raspy smoker's voice. "That girl of yours, Clark ol' boy, is a real spitfire." A wheezy laugh interrupted his speech and threatened to become one of those horrid coughing jags Clark had become all too accustomed to over the trip. Lenny got control, inhaled with a whistle, and continued, "She's worth going back for. I was worried you weren't man enough for her but, hell, this is a good start."

Clark wasn't sure if Lenny's words were meant as a compliment or an insult. Or, if it even mattered anymore. He had come through with the boat.

"Thank you, Leonard." Then with a tag line that bordered on incipient (in case it had been an insult) "You don't now how much your confidence means to me." Damn straight he didn't. The old geezer couldn't keep an eye on the blonde wife he'd bought and paid for. Clark threw a smoldering look Mary Ellen's way. "I'll miss you both. You've been so comforting."

Mary Ellen looked away nervously, coming to her husband's side to make meaningless physical contact.

Clark eyed the sea-worn vessel and took a deep breath. He did not relish a three-hour cruise back to Sava, especially with men who looked as though they'd throw him overboard for his luggage.

Petra!

It was always her. Dragging him down, holding him back. She'd been an albatross around his neck since the day they met. The men looked up and became quiet in unison as he approached. Good, he thought, and when he was close enough to make an impression, he dropped his bags ceremoniously and gave them his *don't-even-think-about-messing-with-me* look. They remained silent for a moment until one of them, a big man with dirt-covered overalls and a shaved head, spoke.

"Hey, ya goin' ta wreck dem sissy shoes on me boat, mon."

***

She was breathing evenly now.

Sleeping. Peacefully, by the look of it, but considering the fall she'd taken on the dusty road, he knew she had to be watched for signs of concussion, woken regularly to monitor speech and reasoning.

He had to admit, as he pulled a soft worn Afghan over her, that he'd entertained the possibility of carrying her to his bed. Well, he sighed inwardly, be careful what you wish for. Careful and a little more specific.

He'd almost gotten her killed. The job had always come first. He'd grabbed her, thinking only of the outcome. Bait. That's all she was. Unexpected, beautiful, and obviously effective bait.

He'd been off the mark with this one. He'd grossly underestimated how effective that bait would be, and how quickly it would be taken. Was he losing his edge? Was that why he'd missed the van on the pier? There were so many transients on the island this time of year, but that was no excuse.

She stirred with a breathy moan. He brushed loose curls away from her face.

He knew why he'd missed it.

***

As much he dreaded returning to Sava, Clark looked forward to leaving this crew of crass marauders behind. He couldn't understand most of what they grunted between each other, but he was obviously the butt of their jokes. It was unbearable. Intolerable. If there was one thing Clark could not abide by, it was chiding by underlings. These men were underlings. The fact that they outweighed him by as much as a hundred pounds each and outnumbered him five-to-one was all that held him back.

In his world, the real world where men shaved and bathed and picked their teeth only on rare occasion and then with manufactured, regulation toothpicks rather than dirty fingernails and serrated ten-inch blades, he would have cut these fools to their knees. When it came to verbal lashings, Clark was among the best. His ravings were known to send a veteran waiter out the back door and a hard-as-nails ticket agent to tears.

He was accustomed to service with a smile. He was not accustomed to bouncing around on a splintered bench, wet from sea spray, all the while being sneered at by men who looked and acted less refined than the bums he sometimes had to swerve around in his Lexus. And to think he'd paid for this pleasure. High-seas robbery.

Unsophisticated robbery when compared to the intricate shifting of money he did for Alexander Trumad back in Minneapolis. And not nearly as risky. In precarious balance was his job as a vice-president at MidWest State Banks. One slip and the federal banking commission would be on him like flies. One slip and he'd be dealing in cigarettes and candy bars with guys named Bubba.

He wasn't about to pound out licence plates at ten cents an hour. Especially since he'd found a way to cut himself in on a little more. He'd thought his cut fair until he'd seen the actual numbers on paper. So, he did the only logical thing. He gave himself a raise.

It wasn't stealing, it was his due. An extra decimal point on the foreign exchange, too minuscule for

Trumad to miss or to attract attention. But there were other glitches. Well ... one.

Petra. That nosy, spoiled little witch, had surprised him with a reality check a couple of weeks ago when she'd told him she'd asked for an audit on an account with large cash deposits that had not been reported to the IRS. An oversight which had been corrected later on, proof of which, falsified of course, he'd gladly supplied. He was not the only one in the country working for Trumad. Fortunately, the numbskulls at the bank had not even come close to untangling the complicated web of bogus accounts and companies he'd strewn across the country. The apology he'd elicited from them for the embarrassment was worth its weight in gold.

He'd expected gratitude when he'd informed Trumad of the incident and got it. Trumad praised his quick thinking. He also arranged for Clark to travel to the Caribbean for the party of the century where they would meet in person and Clark would be rewarded for a job well done. Almost. There was still the issue of ... Petra.

Well, it was her own fault. Really. Sticking her nose where it didn't belong. She was hardly more than a glorified secretary with long lunches and an office as big as his. All because daddy wanted to keep an eye on his precious baby girl, after that *bowler* incident ...

Clark had been working the *Petra angle* for a year now and fully expected to marry into an unfathomably rich family. That would no longer be possible. With Petra out of the picture he'd have to resort to plan B. He'd have to settle for amassing a fortune by way of climbing the ranks of Trumad's organization. In the meantime, he would be the grieving fiancé, always with a special place in Marshall Logan's ... bank.

Clark wasn't keen on *offing* the boss's daughter but

Trumad had made it clear. Petra was a liability they could not afford. She had stumbled across their operation once; she could do it again.

In the moonlight, Clark could make out the long wooden pier he'd sailed from this morning. It was deserted. Quiet. Creepy. What had he expected, a marching band and fireworks? Apparently he was on his own.

The boat pulled up to the dock and, to Clark's horror, anchored several feet out.

"Can't av me girl bumpin' up agin' dat dock."

"How on earth am I supposed to —"

"Don' go wettin' yahself, we gotta ladder."

A ladder? They were a good fifteen feet away from the dock. Clark didn't recall seeing a ladder on board. There was that rope contraption that had clunked against the outside of the hull back in Caracas but, well, he could hardly expect Clark to shimmy across that in the dark, could he? Seriously? What about his luggage?

The Louis Vuitton valise hurled through the moonlight and landed loudly on planking. Before he could utter surprise or disgust, its mate, a matching garment bag, followed, landing next to it.

"Are you out of your mind?" Clark exploded. "That luggage cost more than this thing you call a boat."

The burly, baldheaded man ignored him and threw the end of the ladder, the rope ladder, onto the dock. Metal spurs dug into the planking and glittered eerily in the half-light.

"You are out of your mind," Clark huffed, "if you think, for one minute, that I'm getting on that thing! I paid good money for safe passage."

"You good swimmer?" the man asked, sending his crew into a fit of raucous guffaws. "Toby, show dis one how it done."

At the command, a middle-aged man with knotty

fingers and bowed legs scaled his bulky frame across the rope and wood contraption like a circus chimp.

"Nutin' to it," said the captain with obvious contempt, "for a mon."

For a man? What the hell was that supposed — oh, he knew what it was supposed to mean. Clark panned the faces of the men who'd taunted him for hours and weighed his options.

Climb or swim.

Clark took a steady breath, poised one pig-skin-covered foot and grabbed the first wooden rung with both hands. When it didn't flip over, he relaxed a little and made his way over the water, trying to mimic the man who'd made it look so easy. It wasn't so hard after all.

He felt the heel of his twelve-hundred-dollar loafers miss the wooden rung and winced as the others laughed. For the first time in a long time he did not feel entirely in control. He ignored the cackling buffoons behind him and clung to the ladder as if it were a rich divorcee's checkbook.

FIVE

It had been an hour since the last time she was up.

"Miss Logan," he said, disturbing the peace, "wake up."

She sat up slowly, on an elbow, but her look was vacant. Empty.

"Miss Logan. Do you know where you are?"

Dim light spilled a milky, translucent glow over her. She blinked, as if clearing her eyes, but did not try to find him.

"Do you know where you are?" he repeated more forcefully. She should be able to answer this.

"I'm in your bed," she said in a soft, almost childish voice.

Frans smiled in spite of himself. It was not the answer he had expected, but it was an answer.

"Do you know who I am?" he asked.

"The Burgomaster."

"Very good, Miss Logan. Excellent."

"Do I get a gold star?"

"A gold star?"

She blinked again then turned her wide blue eyes towards him. "A gold star. You know, for remembering."

A little rambling ... not terribly unusual with this kind of injury. Not alarming. She'd snap out of it and probably wouldn't remember a thing in the morning. He'd humor her.

"Oh course," he said, patting her back. "In fact,

Miss Logan, considering the day you've had, I think you deserve two."

"I can't remember it very well," she continued, talking to him, through him, not really seeing him. "What happened?"

"You will," he said simply.

"No," she said, shaking her head, ringlets, almost auburn in the dark room, brushing the skin of his bare arm. "I try, but ... but I can't. Clark told me, but I can't remember."

This wasn't about the men in the van. This was something else. *Martin.*

"What did he tell you?"

"He said ..." She had a far-off look; her lip trembled.

"What did he say?"

"He said I was colder than the water. Like ice. Freezing. No, not freezing." She bit her lip as if trying to sort out the woes of the world, and Frans felt his stomach lurch. "Frigid. Yes, that's it. He said I was frigid. He said I belonged in the lake."

Frans helped her lie down and pulled the blanket back up to her chin. His fingers grazed the bare skin of her arms.

Cold as ice. The moment he thought it, her body began to tremble. Uncontrollably.

He slipped his arm beneath her and, lying down beside her, pulled her into his warmth.

"Shh —" he crooned into the soft, wild curls over her ear. "No one's going to hurt you. I have you now."

***

"Gone? What do you mean, gone?"

The chubby-faced little woman yawned while Clark swallowed his impatience. It was late, sure, but you'd have thought she'd be grateful for the business rather than staggering around in a ratty robe, muttering something in that island lingo under her breath.

"Gone," the woman answered after treating him to a good look at her tonsils. "Gone, gone. Gone away."

"I don't understand," he said, trying to keep his tone firm but low. "Miss Logan was here this morning. She didn't board with me. I know she's still here."

"No," the woman said, revving up for another full-bodied yawn. "She leave today. Gone."

"Where did she go?"

The woman shrugged. Then stretched. There was a hole in the armpit of her robe and he looked away.

"She must have said something."

"No."

Clark looked at her closely in the light of the single fluorescent tube hanging over the reservation desk and tried to read her. Her English was much better a couple of days ago. She'd chatted him up when they'd registered; now all she could do was utter a word here, a word there. She was tired but Clark detected more. She seemed almost secretive. Watching her words. Why would Petra check out? Where would she go? Clark knew with certainty that the *Surf Queen* was the only departing vessel that day.

"I would like a room," he said, reaching for the valise that held his valuables. "The same one as before, if it's available." Oh, yeah, like that was going to be a problem.

"Visa?"

"Yes," he answered automatically, his hand swimming in the bag for his wallet. That was odd. He was sure he'd packed it away in the case so his smarmy shipmates couldn't pickpocket it.

"You av Visa?"

Now she was playing impatient with him. She yawned again and Clark took the opportunity to pull the bag onto the counter and open it so he could see inside. He tossed the contents around, searching for the one thing he knew he would not find. How in the hell had they gotten his wallet? He had sat on his luggage the whole trip. The only time it was out of his reach was when the Captain threw it on the dock and he —

Damn! That hairless ape hadn't been protecting his tub of splinters from the dock. He'd made Clark climb that crummy ladder to distract him so the other guy, the one who'd gone first, could rip him off.

Well, maybe Petra had some —

Gone, gone. Gone away.

Petra didn't have her cards. Or cash. They were still on the *Surf Queen*. Clark hadn't thought to bring them, which, aside from being a huge inconvenience now, was sloppy. He hadn't thought to bring them because Petra would have little use for them, her impending death and all, but that's exactly why he should have. It might look suspicious. As if he knew she wouldn't be needing them. How he hated all this details stuff. Loose ends.

"My fiancée has it," he said, leaning over the counter and smiling apologetically. "We had, well, a little disagreement. I left in a hurry. I need to find her, you see." He looked away in a feigned morose expression that teetered on tear-jerk. "We were supposed to get married today and I — I, excuse me." Clark took a deep breath, bit his knuckles and forged on. "I just don't know what I'll do if I can't find her. She might come back here. She means everything to me. I have to make it up to her."

There was skepticism in the woman's tired eyes, but he saw it give way to pity and seized the opportunity. "You know I'm good for it," he said. "I'll pay more. Extra. Please, ma'am? You're a beautiful woman, some man must have chased after you."

She smiled and he knew he was in.

"Visa tomorrow?" she asked, handing him the key.

"First thing," Clark answered, already halfway up the stairs. He needed a bath, a few hours of sleep and a little information on the whereabouts of Petra, his soon-to-be-once-again (but not for long) adoring fiancée.

Everything was under control.

***

Petra sighed, relishing the comfort of the strong body engulfing hers, the giant limbs steadying hers. Keeping her safe.

It was always like this in dreams. Well, maybe not always. Not her dreams.

She was dreaming, wasn't she?

Petra stirred, feeling her limbs brush the warmth of an apparition she had conjured so perfectly she could smell and hear and —

It wasn't a dream.

How, she wondered half-soberly, had she ended up in the arms of the Burgomaster? The last thing she remembered was the van and the men. Big men. They had —

"Are you awake?" he asked. His voice was quiet. Deep and throaty. It warmed the hair on her cheek.

Was she? Awake?

She didn't want to answer. She was afraid he would disappear into the darkness that surrounded her.

***

"I am," the man with perfect posture and profiles so symmetric he could don a dozen different disguises with an easy, handsome anonymity, spoke out loud to his reflection, "Alexander Trumad."

Self affirmation never hurt.

He never ceased to amaze himself. His plan, simple

but efficient, was now back on track. Channeling currency through any legitimate institution presented a certain amount of risk. Martin had accepted that risk along with a nice percentage of *clean* money. For a smarter man that would have been enough. Clark Martin was not a smart man.

Trumad admired his physique once more, thinking of the pleasures awaiting him in the adjoining room. It had been a while since he'd had a brunette. And that mole. He'd seen all her movies.

Losing his edge? His edge had never been sharper.

SIX

The telephone.

Had it been ringing?

Frans opened his eyes. Moonlight. Half-light. Breathing, not his own. Warmth. Skin. Hair.

Lots of hair.

He smiled and reached for a handful. Silk slipping through his fingers. As if in answer, she stirred. Her lips were so ...

Soft. Softer than he'd imagined. His mouth lingered ... then traced a soft path to her neck. She moaned, easing into his warmth with a familiarity she could not know.

The shrill sound of the phone was almost a relief.

Frans lay still for a moment, gathering his self-control as he stared down at the sleeping beauty, then pulled himself away from her and stumbled into the office, snatching the receiver up on the fifth ring.

"De man is back."

Frans recognized the throaty soprano that belonged to Marta, hotel owner and unofficial news source of the island.

"Martin?"

"Yes. De one she wid before."

It was working. Frans felt the tightness in his neck and shoulders that always proceeded a major bust.

"I tol' him she left, dat's all. Says he love her. I don' tink so. You should hear fight when dey here last time. Bad news, dat one." She whistled into the phone. "You know."

"Thank you, Marta, I owe you big."

"Oh, Frans, you don' wan to give de kinda payment I be wantin," Marta cackled into the phone before hanging up.

Frans ran a wide hand through his tousled hair, pushing it off his face. It would be morning in a few hours. Time to call in the troops.

Petra Logan. Her image drifted into his mind.

He found himself opening the bedroom door, slowly. Noiselessly. Drawn to her by the moonlight caressing her face and spilling over the soft rising of her breasts.

Frans had nothing to offer her but lies.

She was too smart, too headstrong to be satisfied with anything but the truth. She would find out eventually, when all this was over. He wished there was a way to tell her now.

***

Clark was up at the crack of dawn. He was not accustomed to this early riser bit but there were things, one thing in particular, that needed to be done. The earlier, the better.

Clark used his cellular to call his assistants (he refused to consider them associates, knowing he ranked considerably higher with Trumad than either of the two glorified security guards) to get the scoop on Petra. The woman at the front desk had been no help at all other than to tell him she was gone. Gone, gone. Gone away. Well, if she wasn't here, she had to be somewhere. Somewhere close by.

"This is Martin." He spoke loud and slow. "I - am - on - Sa - va." Other than something that sounded like a grunt, and deep breathing, there was no intelligible response. "Clark Martin. Trumad sent me. Remember?"

"Trumad." A man's voice on the other end.

"I need to find Miss Logan, the woman I was staying with."

"Burgomaster."

"What?"

"We try gettin' her for you. Burgomaster come and take her away."

"You mean a cop?" The cop *still* had her? Only Petra could turn a parking ticket into an international incident.

"He take her from us."

"What do you mean, take her from you?"

"We catch her, but den de Burgomaster come. We let her go. Maybe she dead now."

It was too much to hope for. Clark groaned. "I need a car."

"We come."

Clark flipped the phone closed and tossed it on the bed. This was great. Just perfect.

***

Frans woke up at his desk, stiffness greeting his forty-year-old joints. They preferred horizontal slumber. He pulled his fingers through his shaggy mane and massaged his forehead. Light forced its way in, making the transition painful. Sava's first light was always the brightest and deadliest of the day. Before Frans could gather his thoughts chronologically, she filtered into them, shattering what little concentration he'd hoped to hang on to.

The door of the office burst open and Frans looked up. Clark Martin. Crossing the space between them with cocky strides too wide to be natural. Predictable as always. As if it were going to be as easy as Frans handing her over gift-wrapped.

"I need to speak to the Burgomaster."

Frans didn't get up. "I am the Burgomaster," he replied in an official tone. "Take a seat would you, Mr. —"

"Martin. Clark Martin. And I'd prefer to stand."

Frans shrugged, as if to say *suit yourself*.

"I'm here for Petra Logan."

Frans looked up at Martin with a deliberate blank look.

"Petra Logan?" At Fran's continued silence, Clark barked, "Are you deaf? I've come to get my fiancée."

Frans stood slowly, bringing his six-foot-four-inch frame to its fullest. "My hearing is very good, Mr. Martin, it is my patience that is doing poorly. If you have something to tell me, something that might interest me in my official capacity as Burgomaster of Sava, I suggest you take a seat."

Martin's eyes made a quick assessment of Frans, then he perched himself on the very edge of the chair. "Now," Martin continued in a whiny, less demanding tone, "can we get to the —"

"Name?" Frans asked, having already returned to his seat, his pencil poised over a form.

"I already told you my name," Martin protested until Frans looked up. "Martin. Clark Martin."

"Clark with a *C*?"

"Yes, of course with a *C*. How else would you spell it?"

"Mr. Martin, things will go much quicker if you simply answer the questions. I don't have time for a spelling bee. Now this woman, your fiancée, what is her name?"

"You know damn well what her name is," Clark seethed. "You picked her up yesterday."

"I would have remembered picking up someone's fiancée. The bars, they closed early yesterday."

"Not in a bar, you imbecile." Clark jumped out of his seat. "On the road. About a mile or two from here."

"We do not allow the girls to work there anymore."

"She's not a hooker, you moron."

"Why, then, was she working on the road?" Frans stared hard at Clark. "Mr. Martin, Sava takes a very serious view towards, how do you say in America ... pimps?"

"I am not a pimp!"

"Well then why are you here? I did not arrest any ... working girls last night."

"Petra Logan hasn't worked a day in her life!" Clark blurted. "She's my fiancée. It's your job to find her. I have friends in high places and if you don't help me, I'll call them."

Frans slid the black rotary phone across the desk. "By all means. If what you say is true, and I have no reason to believe it's not, then a woman has been abducted, and we will need all the help we can get."

Their eyes met. Locked. It was one split second, but a worthy one. Martin retreated. "She's around here somewhere. I'll find her." He turned, a little clumsily, on his heels and stalked out, slamming the door behind him.

"But you won't get her," Frans said under his breath, pitching the crumpled paper ball across the room and dead center into the trash.

***

What was that?

Petra opened her eyes.

A bed. She was on a bed. A fan clicked above in low speed, pushing the warm air around.

Where? Where was she?

She remembered. Tall, blond. Burgomaster.

Burgomaster Frans Vondel, at your service,

Madam.

He'd been in this bed. With her.

Or had he?

His arms. His warmth. His touch.

His *kiss?*

A finger to her lips. Soft. Something familiar ...

She sprang to her elbows. It had to be a dream! He was her ...

"You're up."

He looked huge in the doorway. A giant in a playhouse.

Giant arms ... holding her. Holding her ... hostage.

Hostage!

Petra threw her legs over the edge of the bed and stood. Her head throbbed.

"Can I get you something?"

"Off this damn island," she answered.

His response wasn't exactly a smile, but close, she thought. She surveyed the wide chest and strong arms, mentally weighing her options and gaging his reaction. His approach was amiable, gentle, and she suspected this had something to do with the condition she'd been in most of the, what, night? Day? How long had she been his *guest?*

"How long have I been ...sleeping?" she asked in an even tone meant to disguise her concern.

"Most of the night."

"Most of the night?" She bit back more words. She wasn't going to open that can of worms. Not now and maybe not ever. "Have you worked things out yet? Am I free to go?"

A large hand grazed his chin and the smile disappeared. "I am afraid things have become ... complicated with this latest incident."

***

"You don' get de girl?"

"Obviously, I didn't get her," Clark seethed, stepping up into the rusty old van's passenger seat. "She wasn't there. You dolts dragged me out here for nothing."

"Burgomaster got her," the driver, the larger, and smarter (like that was much of a contest) of the two men offered in protest.

"Well, he doesn't got —" Clark took a breath, trying to compose himself enough to repeat the obvious in his own words. "He doesn't have her now. For all I know, he never did. If you're trying to undermine my position with Trumad by sending me on some wild goose —"

"Trumad," the second man, a scaled down version of the first, interrupted from the backseat. "Trumad call for you."

Wonderful. Fabulous. Clark yanked his phone from the human paw and flipped it open. "When?"

"You were in dere," the man answered with a huge, meaty shrug in the direction of the jail.

"If I find one call on my bill that I don't recognize, you'll be sorry beyond your wildest dreams," Clark hissed, punching the numbers he knew by heart. He hadn't planned on contacting Trumad so soon, but he knew better than not to call him back.

***

"Incident? Unbelievable!" Petra fumed. "I've been framed for stealing a car, mauled, practically thrown to my death and you have the audacity to refer to it as an *incident*? Oh, I forgot, we're on Sava. It all makes sense now."

The return of the fire-spewing vixen he'd captured yesterday came as a relief. Other than the splitting headache he suspected she'd be sporting for most of the day, Petra Logan was going to be all right. "I'm glad it makes sense to you, Miss Logan, perhaps you could explain it to me. The men who abducted you, who were they and what did they want?"

"Don't you think I should be asking you that since you sent them after me?"

He felt a smile tugging at the corners of his mouth; she would tire even the most diligent of interrogators. "Miss Logan, I am a simple island Burgomaster. I am here to protect the citizens, not terrorize the tourists."

"I have to say, you've been doing a remarkable job. I can't wait to come back!"

"But of course, Miss Logan, in order to return, that would mean you would first have to be free to leave Sava, which at this point you are not."

"Okay, Vondel, let's just cut to the chase. How much will my freedom cost?"

"Less than your life, I hope."

"That makes two of us," she said with a dismissive roll of her blue eyes. "So, tell me, how much does a ... uh driving infraction — oh, I mean, stolen wreck — set a girl back on Sava?"

Frans hid his grin behind a stern grimace. "Miss Logan, precisely how much money do you have in your possession?"

"I have ..." Her mouth stopped in midair. Her eyes cut away.

"Miss Logan, you have no money, no Visa, no jewelry. What could I possibly want from you?"

***

What did he want from her? *What did she have left?*

He was making too much sense all of a sudden. And yet, nothing made sense. Maybe he wasn't after her money, but he was after something. She was sure of that.

"I don't recall ever telling you who I am, Vondel," Petra said, pulling out her trump card. She had him now.

One eyebrow disappeared into the fringe of shaggy blond hair and a grin formed on his wide mouth. "You talk in your sleep, Petra Logan."

She could see ... feel ... his lips. Heat spread across her face. A dream?

SEVEN

"Well, Mr. Martin, your response, at least, is prompt."

Clark cradled the phone to his ear and sunk into the ripped vinyl upholstery, trying to find a response that wouldn't give away how off-kilter he really was. Nothing came to mind.

"I am assuming you have Miss Logan under your wing again?"

"Well, uh ..."

At Clark's stumbling silence, Trumad pressed. "You do have Miss Logan, do you not?"

"It's not my fault," Clark blurted. "It's them. Mutt and Jeff here."

"Mutt and who?"

"They really made a mess of things, Mr. Trumad. Apparently, from what I've been able to translate, they made some bungling attempt to kidnap her, but she got away. Now she's gone. She's not at the hotel and when I questioned the Burg-a-whatever, he claimed he hadn't seen her."

"You do not want the attention of the law."

"I don't?" Clark realized how weak this sounded. "No, of course, I don't. It just seemed a logical place to start."

"A logical place to end up if there is trouble."

He hadn't thought of that. In fact, the thought of getting intercepted by the law, of being arrested, had not occurred to Clark at all until now. This really put a damper on things. "I'll stay low until it's over," Clark reassured. "And it will be over. Soon. I promise you that." Clark heard the conviction in his own voice and reveled in it. He was done playing around.

"I am counting on you," Trumad said. "You must not disappoint me this time."

"I'm with you," Clark answered more to himself than the dial tone.

***

Trumad hung up the phone. Must he hold their hands through everything? He longed for the days when a hit man actually hit.

"Darling," the breathy starlet called from the other room.

"Coming, my dear," he crooned. She was much better in her movies.

***

Sava wasn't exactly, from what she'd experienced during her short but eventful stay, spilling over with amenities, but hot water was among the few they had. Good thing, Petra thought, exiting the steamy bathroom wrapped in an ancient, fading towel. Reeling across an ashy road, lying in the same clothes for half the day, oh, she must have been a real treat. She hadn't even bothered to look in the little mirror over the sink before peeling off her well-worn top and skirt, afraid that a dusty waif might have actually looked back and melted what little resolve she still possessed. She needed that resolve. Among other things.

Clothes.

Vondel had mentioned something about a box of clothes. In the closet. He was vague, and she didn't ask, although it had crossed her mind for a split second to do just that. He had a box of women's clothing lying around. So what? she chided herself. It was no concern to her.

Petra pulled the flimsy rattan folding doors open and found, as promised, some *things*. Quite a lot of things. Women's things. She kneeled on the closet floor and began sifting through the Burgomaster's sordid trophies. Shorts, tank tops, lacy blouses.

How long had he been on Sava? Most men would have a hard time collecting this much memorabilia in a lifetime. What was the Burgomaster, thirty-five? Forty? Well, he'd been busy. Must be the island air.

They varied in size and taste and had belonged, obviously, to more than one female guest. There were swimsuits, sandals and undergarments of every conceivable ... flavor. There were nighties and teddies, and a pair of black stilettos with six-inch heels. Well, he wasn't discriminating. She knew that much.

How did she measure up against the previous visitors who, judging by the sheer bulk of articles, must have filtered through with the ease of a revolving door? She was obviously not as well endowed as some of them. Most of them. Her tastes ran more along the lines of practical than push-up. Still, the way he'd looked at her, his eyes pulling away from hers and sweeping over her body, suggested he found something he liked. She could feel the red spilling into her face as she remembered his look. And something ... more.

He hadn't mentioned the night before and neither had she. Not yet. She wasn't sure, well, she wasn't really sure of *anything*. Except, maybe, that he'd saved her from the two apish thugs that had tried to mug her out in the open.

Sava. Its placidity had seemed almost comical upon her arrival two days before. So much had changed in such a short time. The last things on her mind two days ago were her safety or outlaw status. She'd been an average tourist. Sweating and trying to get off the island as fast as the rest of them.

Clark had been the lucky one. At least he'd made it to the boat.

She didn't want to think about Clark, right now, though not for the reasons she'd have guessed. She had her reasons, yes, but none of them seemed painful anymore, just inconvenient. Her mind dismissed her missing fiancé and traveled back to the man at hand. Frans Vondel. Burgomaster. For the time being, her host.

Host. It sounded more civil than jailer.

Sea Front. What kind of a place was that? A place with water? Lots of water? A sudden chill caused her to pull the towel a little tighter. Well, she'd find out. He was going to Sea Front so ... *she* was going to Sea Front. That was the deal, right? Not that he'd given her a choice. Not that she'd wanted to stay behind at headquarters, alone, bored and maybe a little ... vulnerable, while he went about and did his Burgomaster thing. With Vondel she had, at least, an inkling of what she was up against. Without him, on her own like she was yesterday, well, anything was bound to happen. Almost had.

Near the bottom of the box, just as she was about to give up looking, she uncovered a delicate pattern, yellow flowers on an ivory background. She knew from experience that the warm color would enhance the color of her hair, making it, too, seem warm. Charged. She pulled the piece out of the box and was pleased to find it came in the shape of a dress. A dress with promising dimensions. Without hesitation she stood up, letting the damp towel fall around her feet and pulled the dress over her head, slipping into its

tucks and curves with the same ease its owner must
have experienced. It was, she thought, glancing madly
around the sparse room for a mirror, a perfect fit.

What would Vondel think? she wondered. Was this
the kind of thing a female fugitive sported at Sea
Front?

As simple and predictable as she'd have expected
the lone authority figure of this small providence to
be, she was surprised to encounter the most complicated, frustrating man she'd ever crossed paths with.
His rough-around-the-edges appearance almost
disguised the reality that he, and he alone, was in
charge of things on this island. His island, she thought.
Though she wasn't the type of woman to back away
from a challenge, it was, she admitted, reassuring to
have a man of strong convictions, and physical
superiority, near by.

Just in case.

***

Whoever had left that dress behind, Frans thought,
taking in the redhead with an enormous amount of
appreciation, deserved his undying gratitude.

"Miss Logan," he said, "I see you've found ...
something."

"There was quite a selection, Vondel," she
answered, turning her face up to his so that he could
see the teasing in her eyes. He sensed she had more to
say on the subject. "This must be a busy place."

"It can be," he answered, playing her insinuation
down with an impassive shrug. "Tourist season can be
especially demanding."

The look on her face was priceless. For the first
time since they'd met, Petra Logan was without lingual
artillery. She turned on her heel and walked to the
door, just missing his smile and treating him to a

spectacular view of her long, exposed back and the fiery tresses caressing it.

Some dress, he thought again, gold and red slipping out into the sun. And *she* knew how to wear it.

EIGHT

"*Marshall*," Joan Wherling flew into the office with uncharacteristic drama, sealing the door shut with her back.

Good grief, Marshall Logan thought, what on earth?

"There are some agents out there," Joan spit out in a loud whisper, jerking her head so the blunt grey cut swirled around her face like a fringe. "They want to see you. *Immediately*."

"Agents?" Marshall asked, still not comprehending the impending doom his executive secretary emitted. Had news of the prospective merger leaked already?

She took a deep breath in an obvious attempt to calm herself. "FBI. Two of them. They say it's urgent."

Urgent? FBI? None of this was making sense, least of all Joan's frenzy. "Better let them in, Joan." He watched his secretary of nearly three decades compose herself, smoothing her skirt and hair before giving him a long, ponderous look. She was asking him, without the words, if there was anything she should know. He hadn't held any secrets from her. She seemed to come to the same conclusion and gave him the smile that, even after all these years, made him feel younger than he could ever claim to be. She opened the door.

"Mr. Logan," said the taller of the two men who were dressed remarkably alike and, aside from a few inches in stature, were also similar in physical appearance. Clean shaven, wire-rimmed glasses, and crisp, cuffed, spotless double-breasted blue suits.

Feds, all right.

Marshall leaned his stocky frame over the large mahogany desk, offering a hand. "I am."

"Pleased to meet you, Sir," said Agent One, shaking cordially as Agent Two sidled up for an introduction. "I'm Federal agent Lance Bukupski. This," he released Marshall's hand and took a single step sideways, "is Federal Agent Roger Doer."

"FBI," Marshall said, completing the opening ceremony.

"Yes, sir," Bukupski answered as the two men simultaneously pulled out leather-bound identification for inspection.

"Sit. Please," Marshall said, indicating two red leather chairs adjacent to his desk. "How can I help you gentlemen?"

"Mr. Logan," Doer took the interview baton and leaned forward, his small frame making little impact on the space between them, "we have a rather delicate situation regarding some recent transactions authorized by this institution."

This wasn't about the merger, Marshall thought, his curiosity piqued. "What kind of transactions?"

"The kind of transactions," the agent continued, "where large amounts of unaccounted capital are deposited into legitimate accounts, then moved. Often, out of the country."

Marshall pushed his chair back, aghast at the implication. "Money laundering? Preposterous!"

"Well, that is the phrase commonly bantered around in these circumstances," said Bukupski, in calm opposition to Marshall's outburst. "What we know, Mr. Logan, is that someone working for this institution has had business dealings of a discreet nature and enormous proportion."

"I'll order an audit. We'll get to the bottom of this.

There has to be some kind of mistake."

"We were hoping you'd say that," Bukupski said. "Makes our job a whole lot easier. I guess the warrant won't be necessary."

Warrant? They were serious. *This* was serious.

"Who?" Marshall asked, still not completely convinced.

"One of your vice-presidents," Bukupski said, lowering the boom. "Clark Martin."

Clark?

"That's impossible," Marshall said, losing the feeling in all four appendages. "Now I *know* you've made a mistake. I know Clark personally. He's engaged to my daughter. They're on a cruise as we speak. You're not implying my daughter is involved in this — this misunderstanding?"

"Well, you see, Mr. Logan," Doer offered diplomatically, "that's where this gets a little sticky."

***

So this was it, Petra thought. Sea Front.

Not bad. It was considerably more lush and maintained than anything she'd seen on Sava so far. Vondel swung the old Datsun off the dusty main drag and onto a clean concrete parkway that ended with a touristy-type parking lot. A wide, mowed lawn stretching several hundred feet met up with a well-groomed beach, crowded with thatched umbrellas and sunbathers. The view, slightly elevated from the lot, was outstanding and emphasized the startling hues of water, sand and grass. A modern-looking beach house was perched on a slight incline just left of the swimming area, which was marked off with buoys. Further down the shoreline were two long piers and a smattering of boats.

Petra walked beside Vondel as they made their way across the grassy stretch. The ground was soft, uneven. New grass not yet adhered to the island beneath it. She could relate.

"What's going on?" she asked Vondel as they neared the end of the lush, uncertain grass and came upon a scrubbier version where several groups of islanders were assembling tents and booths.

"Sava's version of Carnival," he answered, his pace slowing a little as he turned towards her. To accommodate her, she wondered, or, was he simply assimilating to the island rhythm? "It's a big celebration. Food, music, games. Finishes up tomorrow night with a dance. Everybody goes. They call it the Barefoot Ball."

She was maneuvering much better on the harder ground. Not that she had needed his help. Not, she thought, watching the way his huge frame move easily with its almost boyish gate, that he'd offered. "Barefoot Ball?" She liked the sound of that. Cinderella minus the glass slippers. "Everybody? Even Burgomaster?"

"Especially Burgomaster," he answered with the slightest impression of a smile forming on his tanned face. Was he teasing her?

"Frans!" A sturdy woman with long grey braids waved him over to her booth. She was stirring something in a tarnished kettle over open flames, with a wooden spoon so large it resembled a paddle. The woman lifted it briefly, then plunged it back in. *It was a paddle.* A strange, pungent aroma greeted them from several feet away. Nearing, Petra watched as the woman offered a paddle-full to Vondel. He didn't even hesitate.

"Your best yet," Frans told the woman who blushed at his compliment.

"Oh, Frans," the woman said, tossing one braid behind her the way a young girl might, "you always sayin' dat."

"I always mean it," he answered, grinning widely.

"Frans ..."

She was flirting with him, Petra suddenly realized, and at this she couldn't help smiling.

Vondel. Shameless.

He turned towards her, a hint of mischief in those grey-blue eyes. "You should try it," he said, reaching for her, pulling her towards him. She had never considered herself a small woman, but next to him, this close ...

The woman held up the spoon, filled with the pink gravy (so much for strict sanitary guidelines) and poked it towards Petra.

"Oh, I — I don't know. I'm really not hungry."

"You said you were starved in the car," Vondel said, then shrugged. "Your words."

His look did not waiver. It challenged.

She *had* said that.

"What's in it?" she asked the woman, edging timorously towards the ladle.

"Good," said the woman. "Go-oo-od."

Petra tipped her head back just far enough to catch the look on Vondel's face. *I dare you.*

It went down smoothly, tasting better than she'd expected. Chowder of some kind. Spicy and kind of chunky.

"She was right," Petra said, proud of herself for meeting his challenge. "What is it? Some kind of stew?"

Vondel laughed, then said something to the woman. They both laughed heartily. "You don't want to know," he said, a hand on her bare back, gently steering her towards one of the piers.

"Of course I do."

His hand slid down her back, seeming almost to linger at her waist before dropping away. Petra was acutely aware of its absence.

"Are you sure, Miss Logan?"

He stopped and raised an eyebrow at her, waiting for her answer. For an instant, she forgot what she'd been saying. Had he noticed her mental glitch? "I've had snails and frogs' legs. I'm not squeamish, Vondel. Whatever the island delicacy is, I'm sure I can stomach it."

"You choose your words," Vondel said. "I'll not deny you that." A sheepish look built itself around his smile. "Goat intestines."

"Ohhh." She tried to keep the lurch in her stomach from knocking her off her feet. "Of course, *goat intestines*." As if she had them on a regular basis. "Is *that* all?"

"Brains too. Not much goes to waste here."

She felt warm.

"The air is better on the pier," he said, his accent unable to conceal his obvious amusement. "You look a little pale."

The light breeze played with strands of sun-bleached hair, giving him a boyish look. The kind of boy, she knew with an odd certainty, that played jokes on little girls.

***

A reggae beat wafted from the pier and her wide blue eyes came alive, dancing with the music, her wan pallor vanishing. Frans watched her taking in everything around her. Red curls bounced from her shoulders as she turned to acknowledge the stares and greetings of locals who were struck by the unusual, fiery beauty. He knew what they were feeling. He had a hard time looking away himself.

"Much better in person," a man's voice called out in the clear unmistakable language of Frans's first home. "You didn't mention *that* when you called."

Frans greeted the agent in Dutch. "You didn't ask."

Though officially under the sovereignty of the Netherlands, Sava's population had but a handful of Dutch-speaking natives. English was the most useful with tourists. For this reason Frans and Rolphe could speak in virtual privacy anywhere on the island.

Petra eyed them curiously but said nothing. For all she knew, he was conversing, as the Burgomaster, with a local.

"The agency is backing you on this —" Rolphe's eyes traveled the length of Petra. He grinned. "Development. Especially since the lover returned. They've already brought Foley and Andrews back."

"Trumad is coming," Frans answered, nodding. "I can feel it."

"You and your feelings. Well, they seem to be paying off."

Frans shrugged at Rolphe and then turned to Petra. "He says you are very beautiful."

She looked away, smiling to herself. Surely she was used to hearing the words. She couldn't know they were his.

"Frans, you dog," Rolphe scolded with a scruffy laugh. "Seriously, I have some pretty big stuff."

"About our friend."

"About *her* friend," Rolphe corrected, nodding towards Petra. "The lover."

The lover, Frans thought with more animosity than he'd expected. Petra came closer, curiosity over their conversation obviously killing her. Frans smiled. "He wants you to look at his chickens."

"Really?" she asked, crouching down next to the matching set of wire cages. "Any particular reason why?"

"He's just getting to that," Frans answered.

"The lover is a dead man. He's been skimming. Not much. A little here, a little there but you know our old friend Trumad ... he doesn't like to share." Rolphe stopped, giving Petra a glance before giving Frans a hard stare. "It was supposed to be a double hit. The girl and the lover. The only promotion awaiting him is a trip to the next world, by way of suicide likely — the grief-stricken fiancé unable to cope with her unfortunate drowning. It's thin, but it might have worked."

Still crouched down with the chickens, fiery tendrils spilling over the curve of her bare back, she startled Frans with a look so exposed, so open, anger flooded his senses. Trumad. Martin. Most of all, himself. They were all using her. Two days ago, this wouldn't have bothered him. What had changed?

He addressed the pretty, upturned face. "What do you think?" Forces had been set in motion that he was now powerless to stop, but at least he could protect her. He smiled devilishly. He might as well make the best of it.

"I think ... they're chickens," she answered. A perfectly arched brow told him she was at a loss. He liked her this way. Unguarded. Hanging on his every word.

"He wants to use them as payment," Frans said, avoiding Rolphe's face.

"For what?" she asked.

"You."

***

"What did they want?" Joan asked in a whisper even after the elevator doors closed behind the agents.

"Clark. They think he's involved in something," Marshall answered, not sure how much to tell Joan. He hadn't decided, yet, how much he knew. Or believed. He needed proof.

"What kind of something?"

They'd been together a long time. If there was anyone at the bank he could trust, a concept that he would have to reexamine in light of this incident, it was Joan. "The FBI thinks he's been cleaning money for someone."

"Are they certain?"

Joan's tone did not reflect the shock Marshall thought this information should warrant. She was the eyes and ears of this seven-floor building, MidWest's corporate head office, and seemed to know everything going on in the company, both on a personal and professional level. The large commercial banking branch on the first two levels where Clark earned his keep by, among other things, managing the branch's biggest accounts, was no exception. Had she suspected?

Had he?

"I need to see all Clark's records. Every account. Every transaction." How many could there be? Marshall thought. These were things generally delegated to subordinates.

NINE

"What do you mean," Petra asked, standing up suddenly, hands on hips, nostrils flaring, *"for me?"*

Frans held back his smile, not an easy feat in this circumstance. She was a smart woman and he was certain she drew the full meaning of the situation — as he'd presented it. Her body, so fluid and full of bounce just seconds before, was rigid in defiance. Her eyes blazed.

"They are not bad," he said, crouching down to examine the livestock Rolphe carted around as props in their undercover facade. He purposely avoided her eyes. "I've seen worse."

"Vondel," she insisted in a conspiratorial whisper, "you don't mean? He doesn't think —"

"He thinks you are quite beautiful," Frans said, repeating the sentiment he'd relayed earlier. She'd been flattered then. She was alarmed now. Alarm played well on her, enhancing the already dramatic features of a pretty and unusual face. "And he's willing to pay for you."

"I'm not a — a" she stuttered, then flashed Rolphe a quick, disarming smile. "Tell him I'm not for sale."

Frans stood and took her in. Her red mane was no match for the flames that leapt from her eyes. "I'm sorry, Miss Logan, but it's not that simple."

Rolphe was enjoying himself and giving her a lecherously amorous ear-to-ear grin.

"What this gentleman wants is a little more permanent than ..." he stretched the words out playfully, as if the subject matter was delicate and difficult to banter about between the two of them, "a single encounter."

"I don't understand," she said.

Frans didn't believe it for a second. "He would like you to be his, ah, how would you say this in your country?" Frans rubbed a huge palm over his stubbled chin. "Woman."

"He wants to *marry* me?" she gasped in controlled horror, all the while keeping the leering, grinning Rolphe in her sights.

"Perhaps," Frans offered hopefully, "in time."

She moved close to him. The lesser of two evils, he mused.

"It is customary for a woman of your availability," he peered down into her blue, worried eyes, "to consider all serious offers."

"I — I will." She quickly amended, "I mean, I have. Tell him, I'm not interested. I'm not available."

"Maybe not for me," Rolphe chortled in Dutch, "but she looks plenty interested in you."

"What's he saying?" Petra demanded.

"He wants to see the man."

"What man?"

"The one you belong to."

"This is ridiculous," she countered. "I don't owe him any explanations."

"Clearly," Frans said, "you have little knowledge of Savan customs. They are as binding to the local population as law. If you cannot produce proof of your man, and since you are of marriageable age you are considered ... how do you say? Up for grabs."

"I don't believe this! Up for grabs? What about you?" she asked in desperation. "You don't have a wife, do you? Tell him I belong to you."

It was all Frans could do to keep the smile at bay.

"Tell him I'm with you. He'll take your word.

You're the Burgomaster."

"Well, I suppose I could but ..."

"But what?" Panic played with the pretty face.

"I'll be at the boat tonight," Frans told Rolphe. "We've got to set up. Be ready."

"I'll be in touch," the agent answered. "This could be it."

Wide-eyed, she watched the exchange between them, not understanding a word of it.

"Well?"

"He's not convinced," Frans said, taking in the long legs, taut in their wide, stubborn stance. "But," he added, deliberately avoiding the blue eyes that sought his out, "I have an idea." He reached for her, one hand circling her back, and pulled her into him.

***

Out of her control. That was the only way to describe it. Completely, totally out of control. The way she had to force each breath in, then out. The spasms that tightened her chest until she thought she could not breathe at all. She felt hot. Cold. It happened so fast and yet, it was like slow motion. From the moment she realized he would kiss her to the sensation of his lips brushing hers was a small forever. So strange. Absorbing. There was this *thing*. With them. Everything else disappeared. Every doubt, every fear. The people, the noise. Everything. His hands moved up the back of her neck, his fingers lost in her hair. His mouth opened hers. Deep. Long. Moving together. This was it. For now. For as long as it lasted.

He didn't pull away. Not all at once. He brushed his lips softly against hers before pulling back. Still in his arms, she tried to recover. To breathe. To stand. Her feet were on the planks beneath her; she could feel them, but she wasn't sure they could hold her.

"Like a charm," Vondel said.

Like a charm? Her? Them? What did he mean? She didn't trust her own voice. It was all she could do to look at him. Again. She could feel his hand on her back. The other one had gone to his face, pushing the blond strands clear of blue-grey eyes.

"It worked," he said and this time she forced herself to concentrate on his words instead of the hard chest and strong arms. "He's gone."

It worked.

The kiss. That's what he'd meant. That's what it was. Nothing more than a vehicle to discourage an aggressive admirer who was within his *Savan* rights to surrender livestock in pursuit of her. And, surveying the spot the cages and man had just occupied, she could agree. The man was gone. The chickens were gone. It had worked.

Like a charm.

He was smiling down at her.

Petra pulled free and turned away. She'd only been following his lead. It was *his* idea. He'd kissed her.

She'd kissed back but, well, it was part of the act.

Just like the spinning ground and the catch in her throat? The loss of oxygen and the way his fingers seemed to burn her everywhere they touched? Was that all part of the act? If it was, she should be up for an Academy Award. She'd almost fooled herself. What, she wondered, feeling a little foolish, did Vondel think?

"Good," she replied finally.

"I'll say," he said. He was so ... sure of himself. Smug.

"I mean, good thing it worked," she added quickly. Of course that's what she meant. What did he think she meant? "Your methods are a little unconventional," she said, safe, stilted words falling off her lips and into the space between them, "but the results speak for themselves. I suppose I should thank you."

"That is not necessary, Miss Logan." He resumed the walk, strolling further down the pier at a leisurely clip she could keep up with. "If you ask me, the offer was not a particularly generous one, and I would have had to advise you against accepting it had you been so inclined."

Dismissing the notion that she would ever be so inclined, she considered the first part of his statement. What did he mean, *not particularly generous?*

"Not that I care," she said, inching closer, falling into step, "but how much was he offering for my ... companionship?"

"Ten chickens."

"I can count the stupid chickens," she said, trying to keep the impatience out of her tone, "I just don't know how much they're worth on Sava."

"Did you happen to notice, Miss Logan, what condition the birds were in?"

Condition? Live or frozen were the only two she was aware of. "They were in excellent condition," she lied firmly. Yeah, like she would know.

Vondel stopped, a serious look dismissing the boyish, playful one. "Yes, I believe they were at that. Well, considering their size and obvious vitality I would have to say ..." Huge tanned fingers pushed a stray curl from her eyes. "In American dollars?"

She stood stalk still, aware of his touch but refusing to let it derail her thinking. "Yes, of course, in American dollars." Since joining her father's bank, she'd exchanged currency from numerous sovereigns, none of them foul.

"Oh, I think ..."

She could see the wheels at work behind the tanned, rugged face.

"Ten dollars. Give or take."

"Ten dollars?" She shouldn't lose her cool, she knew, over something so ridiculous as the scruffy chicken man and his misguided not-overly-generous bid, but it was impossible. She had to defend her marketability. It was all she had. "*Ten dollars?* I don't believe you."

"That is, of course, your privilege."

His manner was polite, almost overly so. If he was playing with her, again, she couldn't tell. Perhaps he felt a little pity for her garnering such a paltry poultry offer.

Oh, why should she care what he thought? Still ...

"So, what about a — a kiss?" she asked clumsily. "A *real* kiss. Well, how many chickens would that be worth? Ballpark figure."

"You would be ... participating?"

"Oh, for argument's sake, let's say — yes."

"Madam," Vondel said, stroking her cheek in a single easy gesture, "if word gets out I think we will have a bird shortage on the island."

TEN

Well, well, well, thought Clark, peering around a musty canvas wall, so the ice princess was melting. Not much of a feat in this ungodly heat. Nevertheless, one he'd been unable to pull off. Well, maybe if he'd had a little more time with her ...

The Burgomaster was a liar and a cad. A foul man, all in all. Clark grimaced at how easily he'd let the blond monster intimidate him back at the jail. Petra had been there all along. Not only had the cop lied about her being there, he'd gone ahead and put the moves on her *after* Clark informed him that Petra was his fiancée. Some men, he fumed, had no scruples. Clark wondered if the Burgomaster got a hearty chuckle out of it. If they both did.

The thought made his blood boil. Boiling blood was not something he needed right now. Clark dabbed a handkerchief across his damp forehead and shifted from foot to foot until his clothing became *unstuck*.

Clark turned. He had the eerie feeling *he* was being watched. A quick inspection of what served as *grounds* (sod rolled out like cheap carpet) proved him wrong. He was probably just a little paranoid. Who wouldn't be?

Clark was eying his surroundings suspiciously as he stepped forward, taking in everything — *except* what was right in front of him. The women and the chickens. Stoneware, ceramic pots, hanging baskets,

T-shirts.

He landed on a rickety table before hitting the ground, taking everything with him. Then he was in the middle of it. The ruckus. The cackling and shoving match that swallowed him up.

A few tacky articles less to unload on tourists and you would have thought the world had come to an end. It wasn't like he'd deliberately knocked it all over. Or the woman. Or the huge kettle of whatever that stuff was. He'd tried to apologize but that woman, the one who'd broken his fall, started screaming as if he'd attacked her. *As if*.

A volatile exchange began between two men standing above him. They seemed to have forgotten him, their displeasure for each other eclipsing Clark's involvement, and he took full advantage. Careful not to disturb them, Clark found a hole in the forest of legs and rolled through it with an agility he usually saved for *one-on-one* encounters. Without a thought or a look back, he straightened up and brushed the sand off his clothes.

Where was she?

Clark scoured the crowd as he made his way to the pier. They (his alarmingly unfaithful fiancée and the blond ape she couldn't seem to keep her hands off of) had been headed towards it when Clark was detained by the disgruntled island misfits. They couldn't have gotten far, he thought, trying to blend into the crowd.

"Dere he is!"

Instinctively, Clark knew they meant him. His escape, seeming successful, had only been temporary. He had no choice. Blending in was no longer an option. Breaking into a run, Clark made his way down the pier.

***

"What's all that about?" Petra asked Vondel. Jeers and shouts blazed up the pier, directed, she thought a little anxiously, towards them. His arm circled her protectively and she leaned into him.

"Vondel?" It was coming up on them. The noise. The people. A whole throng, with arms waving, words flying. Whatever it was, it didn't look good. A stampede. A riot.

Wordlessly he tried steering her out of the path. His arms were wrapped around her now and she huddled close, slipping one of hers around him. They could weather a hurricane like this, she thought, feeling secure in his —

Pushed. Pulled. Hair. Feet. Hands. Stomped. This way, that way. Moving him away.

"Vondel!" she screamed. "Vond —"

Twisting, staggering, she was flung from the ruckus. Free of the madness, she searched the crowd anxiously for the Burgomaster.

A glimpse of blond bobbed above the mass.

Vondel.

He was coming for her.

The crowd spilled to both edges of the pier, forcing Petra to back up sea side towards the longest and furthermost point of the pier in order to avoid the out-of-control throng. Her chest tightened as she realized how close she was to the water. Deep. Dark. She closed her eyes and inhaled, trying to ease away the uncontrollable fear. As long as she was careful ...

***

He was getting good at this.

Once more, Clark had managed to elude the wrath he'd created. Scurrying away on splintered knees, he looked up just in time to make a startling, fascinating discovery. Petra Logan was ten feet away.

She wasn't going back to the hotel with him. The cop, making his way out of the mob, had robbed Clark of any possibility of that. The *happy-couple* guise Trumad had ordered, meant to dismiss suspicion over Petra's impending accident, was not happening. The red-haired albatross had picked now, in this of all places, complete with the brutish blond neanderthal, to overcome her little ... problem.

Trumad wasn't going to be happy. Clark had a way with women, there was no denying that, but there was only so much he could do. Trumad would find out eventually. Clark would probably have to tell him.

Or ... maybe not.

She was going to go in anyway. He'd be saving Trumad time and trouble. It wasn't his fault she couldn't swim or keep her nose out of his business. A nudge. A bump. Hardly murder, more like ... an accident.

She was standing right on the edge. Perched, actually.

When opportunity knocks, Clark thought, positioning himself in a runner's stance, you don't wait for the doorbell.

It was a clear hit. His shoulder, her back. The jeering crowd of island misfits muffled his steps. She never knew what hit her.

He hit her, of course. Right on target. Perfect. A clear, hard hit that knocked her off her feet and right into the depths of what she feared most. She didn't have a chance. He could have been a linebacker if that coach back at St. Johns hadn't had such a chip on his shoulder over that little thing with his daughter. He wished Coach Weasel-Face Smithers could see him now. He'd knocked the ice princess a good ten feet off the pier. If only, he thought as gravity kicked in, he'd kept it to five feet. Five feet and he'd still be on the dock.

***

The sensation of falling was over so quickly it hardly compared to the sensation of drowning. A painful jolt, a moment of flailing limbs uselessly searing through space. Nothing next to certain death.

I'm drowning, Petra thought, going under. Again. She didn't know how many times she'd gone down, only that she was powerless to stop. Each time she came up slower, went down sooner. She was petrified. Dark. Alone. She couldn't breathe. She was ... drowning.

Not again. No! No! No-o-o!

Her limbs moved without consent. Survival instinct. But her instincts were wrong. She was going down. She needed something to hold on to. Last time she'd had ... something. A float?

No, last time she'd had Clark.

***

"This is the end of it!" Frans declared, settling the matter, whatever it was, in a tone so penetrating, so deadly, even those who did not speak English pulled away from each other, allowing the clamor to dissipate. "One more incident like this and Carnival is over! Do you understand?"

He heard the *aye's* and other mumbled agreements and took it on faith or, at least uneasy optimism, that his threat would ward off future antics of this magnitude. Shading his eyes, Frans peered over the heads of the crowd trudging away, looking for the woman who'd clung to him moments before. He could still feel the fire where her body had pressed into his.

She was gone.

Had she wandered away to explore the grounds, observe the locals? Or, had she ignored his warnings and gone off to find an ally in her quest to depart Sava?

He allowed himself another thought. Had his kiss alarmed her? This was a job. Official business. Lives were at stake. Especially hers. What had come over him?

Where was she?

"Rolphe!" he called across the pier to the agent up-righting his squawking, caged birds. "Did you see where she went?"

"She was right over —" Rolphe returned in Dutch, an outstretched hand gesturing towards the end of the pier. "There?" Rolphe looked around, confused. "I just saw her, Frans."

Something was wrong. Frans could feel it.

He ran down the pier, shoving past the stragglers. Rolphe had just seen her, but —

Something was wrong.

His pulse raced in his head, nearly exploding.

***

Petra fought the thing that came from nowhere and circled her throat. With what little strength she had left and fingers she could not feel, she tore at it. It was strong. It pulled her. Some sort of sea monster, she thought as the darkness closed in. Perfect. Just ...

***

The struggle, her clawing, transformed the rescue into a wrestling match. She was stronger than she looked.

Terrified, she flung her arms about erratically. Frans constricted the twisting, wrenching form from behind to limit the flailing of her limbs. He shouted out her name over the splashing water and her own immersed cries, but it didn't help. She was fighting something. Something more than the water. Frans knew it as instinctively as he'd known where to find her. Petra Logan was in a place he couldn't get to, and she was fighting for her life.

With hard, forceful kicks Frans pulled her towards shore. More than halfway back, he felt her body go slack. He had to get her out of the water. Now.

His feet found the soft bottom. Her limp form folded into his chest, he forged out of the water with an urgency he'd never known and dropped to his knees onto the hot sand.

His mouth pressed over hers and blew in air. Her lips, barely parted, were still. Cool. He would give anything at this moment to feel them move against his. Quiver ...

The barest movement. A shudder. Frans felt it in every part of his body. She was breathing.

Soft shallow intakes of air slipped through the full, pink lips, her breasts pressing against him in a gentle rise. He loosened his grip, slipping one hand into the wet, tangled mass of hair. Closed lids twitched then fluttered, protecting precious sapphires. On crouched legs, Frans shifted so that he blocked the afternoon sun with his back.

She stirred in his arms. A reborn vibrance bled slowly into her, cutting each feature more clearly, more unique, than he remembered. He was hypnotized by the transformation. When her eyes opened, slow and uncertain, he felt relief so great it racked through him with one solid blow.

***

Her eyes were tired. So tired.

"You're going to be fine."

She blinked at the words, trying to focus on their owner. Close. Somewhere over her. Somewhere ... before. She'd been here before. The water. The words. She was sure of it.

I'm saving your life!

"Chl-arhk," she slurred the name.

No. That wasn't right. She was warm. She was safe. It wasn't Clark, it was ...

Her eyes focused on a face hovering over hers. Wide, strong. Tanned.

"Von-del." The name lingered on her lips. She could see him clearly now. His blue eyes were tight around the corners, a crease settled between them. "What ... where?"

A smile pushed out the corners of his mouth. "Rest now." His arms tightened, drawing her deeper into his warmth. He'd done this before, held her this way.

She should say something. Tell him someone had pushed her. Into the water. Hard.

The words wouldn't come. Her limp, used-up body wouldn't stir. Spasms invaded her limbs like electrical jolts and still she couldn't move.

His skin was feverish, warming her body in the places it touched. She should try again. To speak. To move.

Petra took a deep breath. Then another. She drew in as much air as it took to fill her lungs. It was painful, wrenching, but she couldn't stop the pattern. Her body was saving itself.

"She will be fine," Frans announced to the handful of spectators. "I will see to her."

Would she be fine? The pulsing in her head had died down, and she could feel her hands and feet.

Move her fingers.

"Can you stand?"

"Yes," she said without considering an alternative. "Of course."

It was an awkward gesture, but she accomplished it without his help. The sandy world around her rocked for a split second but did not spin. "See? I'm fine."

He smiled, a little heartier now, though the furrow between his eyes remained. "It's time to leave," he said with a gentle but sturdy hand to her elbow.

She allowed herself to be led, tears pricking the corners of her eyes. This — this thing with near drowning and the men who saved her was getting to be entirely too much.

ELEVEN

It was a conspiracy.

How hard could it be to knock off a stranded female tourist? Clark speculated, pulling his water-logged body from one massive pier support to the next.

"Harder than I thought."

Clark hesitated a moment, not really expecting an answer and not sure where, exactly, it had come from. Then he recognized the voice.

Lunatics talk to themselves. Lunatics and senile old bags like his great-aunt Katherine. He intended to inherit money, not traits, from his crazy aunt, but maybe he should watch himself in the future. This *situation* was testing his sanity.

Clark's feet touched bottom and he slunk towards shore in wet sagging clothes. How many times in his lifetime was he going to have to do this?

Watching that sorry excuse for a cop drag his fiancée out of the sea was like driving past a bad accident; as disgusting as it was, you couldn't help but look. That cop was developing a habit of ruining things.

By now Petra should have, courtesy of one of Trumad's hired guns, taken a fateful midnight stroll on deck, resulting in one less passenger at the breakfast buffet, and Clark would have played the confused, somewhat-concerned fiancé looking for his missing bride-to-be.

It would have gone off so well.

Petra's lifeless body would have been a hundred miles back by the time they came to the conclusion that it was the only place it could be.

Walking away from the pier and pulling his soaked golf shirt up over his head, Clark could imagine, clearly picture even, his reactions to each step of the original plan, had it not been foiled by Petra. As clearly as if he were watching it on a screen, he could see himself moving hurriedly from one group of passengers to the next. "Have you seen Petra this morning? No? My, that's odd, neither have I. I wonder —" Then, when confusion had enough time to fester, concern: "Something just isn't right. I need to check her room. This isn't like her." Upon realizing the inevitable, his face screwed up in excruciating, heart-wrenching pain, he'd cry, "No! No! No, it can't be! I don't believe it! No! No! No! No!" Okay, maybe he could come up with something a little more original than *no*, but it was the emotion that mattered, not the words. Besides none of it mattered now anyway.

She hadn't gotten on the boat. And she'd been so close. His brilliant idea of dragging her hordes of luggage aboard had worked, but that stupid, stupid cop ...

Well, what's done was done. Or, in this case, yet to be done.

His moment of inspiration had almost worked. Would have, if the Burgomaster had stuck to his job and attended to the riot at hand rather than jumping in after Petra. Neither of them was being cooperative and this annoyed Clark to no end.

Next time it would be different.

***

"What happened?" Frans asked once the Datsun had pulled away from the smooth ride of blacktop and onto the shock-resistant road. He had a pretty good idea but needed confirmation. She remained withdrawn, her eyes down, her hands loosely clasped in her lap. It was hard to believe this was the same woman he'd brought to Sea Front.

"You don't want to talk about it?" he asked, trying to draw her out.

"Someone pushed me."

Though it was what he expected to hear, the anger still surprised him. He stiffened, gripping the wheel, using every bit of restraint he had to appear calm. Martin? Thugs? He wouldn't alarm her. What good would it do? Besides, as angry as he was with the perpetrator, it was nothing compared to the anger he felt for himself. He should have known.

He hadn't thought for even a moment that someone would be stupid enough to try and *off* her in public, in broad daylight, right under his nose. But that was the problem; he wasn't thinking, he was ... distracted.

"You don't believe me," she said. Her blue eyes met his for a second. "I didn't think you would."

"I believe you but," Frans answered. It was important she not panic. Especially now. "Those men, they were very rowdy. Perhaps one of them stumbled and —"

"No! Someone pushed me, Vondel. Deliberately!"

Frans's eyes left the road and looked directly into her troubled ones. Lying was just part of the job, a part that was now eating up his insides. "You are understandably upset, but —"

"Upset? I almost drowned, Vondel. I just want to go home. Isn't there something you can do? I don't think I'll last another day on this island."

He had no words of comfort. Only the truth could do that, and he cursed himself for having to keep it from her.

***

"What do you mean, he tried to *kill* her?" Manicured but masculine nails drummed the teak desk violently as he spoke into the phone.

"He push her in water. Wham! Just like dat. She go down, way down, but he — Burgomaster — he see her and he —"

Alexander Trumad slammed a fist against the wood desk and rose from his leather-upholstered chair so quickly it rolled into the wall behind him. "That was not," he spit out each word with equal force, "the plan!"

"He get away, Mr. Trumad. He swim away."

"Where is he now?"

"He go to hotel."

"Did anyone see it happen, besides you?"

There was no immediate response and, already infuriated, Alexander bit his lip so hard it drew blood. He heard muffled voices and knew Bernard had his hand over the receiver, consulting, no doubt, with his partner, the equally sophisticated Alphonse. These men were unbearable. This was the last time he recruited amateurs.

"Alphonse, he say, no. Just us."

"Not even the Burgomaster? What about the woman?"

More background chatter, clarity diluted by a meaty palm. "No. She not see. Not him also. Dere was big fight and de Burg —"

"I don't need you to relive the incident, Bernard," Trumad snapped wearily. "I need you to keep an eye on Martin. Don't let him get anywhere near the woman."

"You should tell him," Bernard puffed hesitantly, "he don' much like what we say."

"Oh, for the —" Alexander took a deep breath,

blew it out, and formed clear, calm words the newest additions to his team could understand. "I will call Martin myself and tell him he is to cooperate with you. Apparently Mr. Martin has taken it upon himself to disregard my wishes. I need the two of you to make sure it does not happen again."

"We are de same as him?" Bernard asked enthusiastically.

Alexander hadn't a clue what the man was asking. "Come again?"

"We are de same as Martin. He not boss?"

Never, *ever* again. Alexander sighed. "Yes, Bernard. You and Alphonse and Martin are all equals. In fact," he said, rubbing a hand over his face, soft from the avocado facial he'd had this morning, "you and your cousin actually outrank Martin, though I'd prefer we keep this piece of information between the three of us. You know. *Americans.*"

Alexander heard the men engage in a rapid, foreign exchange and presumed they were congratulating themselves on their promotion. He paced impatiently. "So," he said, finally tying up the loose ends so he could end this call and make another, "your duties are clear? You understand what I want?"

A booming baritone, full of new-found confidence answered, "Yes, boss! We stay wid Martin and keep him from woman so he don' kill her no more."

"Perfect," he said, pushing the *end* button on the portable in front of the big antique mirror. In the reflection was a forced, tight smile that did nothing to placate his mounting apprehension.

***

The first indication that there was any truth to what the agents had told him came by way of a paper mountain. Marshall Logan could not believe how many accounts Clark was handling personally, or how much activity they generated.

"There's more," Joan told him, depositing another sheaf on his desk. "I'm still printing."

Opening and emptying a variety of accounts, none of them financially significant standing alone, seemed to be the focus of Clark's banking duties. Marshall Logan groaned inwardly, comparing the statements. How had this gone on for so many months without anybody finding out?

Well, somebody had found out. Somebody with more banking savvy then any of them would have guessed. Petra. Curiosity had always been a big part of her nature. Marshall could only hope it wouldn't get her in any more trouble. Romping around the Caribbean with a money launderer was more than Marshall's heart could take.

Still, something was bothering him. Something else. They hadn't told him everything.

"Joan, get me the foreign exchange reports," he called out.

***

"I don't care what Trumad told you," Clark said with a deliberate, exuberant authority even the goons who'd been chauffeuring him around the irksome little island should get, "or, what you *think* he told you, I'm the one calling the shots."

"Trumad," Beast number one (Barney, was it? Something like that.) spat some primitive attempt at English, "say: go wid Martin. Stay all de time wid him."

Stay all de time wid him? Trumad?

Hardly, Clark thought. Just another example of how

these two screwed things up. Lucky for Trumad, he was on board.

"I'll-call-you," Clark said, holding his cell phone up, reverting to a slower, more paced form of language that they could, maybe, get right. Understand. "You-come-then."

Confusion crossed over the big men's faces and Clark sighed. "Never mind," he said, climbing out of the old van, tugging his soggy madras shorts out of the gaping crack in the vinyl seat. "Just stay put."

***

The car labored up a steep incline, presenting the shore as smooth beige edging to the softly shifting shape of water.

Water.

Petra shuddered.

Why was this happening? She bit her lip to try to contain the surge of panic that rushed to the back of her throat and stung her eyes. How could she have known, as recent as yesterday morning, that her life was a commodity she would no longer be able to take for granted? To think she'd been so distressed over the absence of her American Express Card. It seemed foolish now compared to what she might have lost.

The men on the road. She'd been so wrapped up in her petty little problems, she'd considered them little more than a nuisance. That had been a mistake. A near fatal one.

And now this.

For a year she'd been struggling with two handicaps, both of which traced back to her first date with Clark. A sailing date. The storm. She'd done everything the doctors had told her to do, but nothing seemed to work. This had been the last step. A last-ditch effort to reclaim the sanity that seemed to have deserted her that disastrous afternoon in May, leaving her to battle, alone, the dreams, the agonizing flashes of doom that woke her regularly. A cruise would put her in close proximity of water and help her over her fear of it. It was supposed to work the same way with Clark. How simple it had sounded. How reasonable. Now, here she was. Clark had deserted her and she'd nearly drowned. She was going backwards, it occurred to her as a single tear slid down her cheek.

She'd never hurt anyone. She paid her bills and obeyed the law. Well, most laws. The ones she knew about. She blinked back the wetness and stole a glance at Vondel, the mysterious foreigner.

He'd detained her for stealing an old car that was nearly worthless and insisted she stay behind, penniless and disposed, until the ridiculous matter was straightened out. Then, he rushes to her side, saving her from thugs and accusing her of ... what? He'd never really said. But he'd alluded to her involvement in ... something.

It was never quite clear with him. Half of what he told her sounded like her own words turned around. He had to know something. More than what he'd told her. Something serious. When he'd warned her she might be safer with him than without him, what had he really meant? Was it the kind of warning he extended any female tourist/felon traveling alone on Sava, or had it been directed specifically at her?

Two incidents in two days was her answer.

She had no reason on earth to trust Vondel. He was little more than a stranger. A stranger who had saved her life. Twice. Which gave her every reason to trust him.

The little car changed strategy, nearly coasting until it leveled out. Skillfully, Vondel swung it off the road and onto a flat, hard patch of earth. Motor still running, he turned to her. "Petra, it's going to be all right."

Before she could respond, he was out of the car and crossing over to her side.

She hoped he was right.

***

Marshall stared at the mess of numbers before him in shock. The little piece of information the FBI agents had neglected to share struck terror through him.

Clark Martin was in deep, deep trouble. It was one thing to have the law after you for funneling dirty money through the country. It was something else entirely to have a crime lord after you for helping yourself to that money. Skimming, it was called.

It was also a death warrant. Clark Martin had signed his own. Marshall could live with that. What he couldn't live with, what chilled his blood and propelled him out of his chair like a shot, was the possibility that Martin might have done the same for his daughter.

"Joan, get me the first flight out," Marshall ordered, a hysterical quality to his voice he'd never heard before. "I'm going to the Caribbean."

"Marshall," Joan said from behind her desk, "all of this seems so, well, are you sure? About going like this? I got the impression the agents wanted you to stay put. And the audit. You should really be here for that."

"You'll handle it, Joan. Act in my behalf. You have my number if something comes up. This thing with Petra, well, you know my daughter as well as I do." A wan smiled crossed his lips. Joan had been something of a surrogate mother and female confidant to Petra since her mother's death. "She's in trouble."

What was it those agents had said that had set off the alarm in his head? Something about Petra and, oh yes—

"Don't worry," they'd told him. "She's in protective custody with one of our best men."

"Protective custody?" Marshall had inquired. He hadn't liked the sound of that. Doubted, highly, anything with the word *custody* in it sat well with his daughter. "What's that? What does she have to do?" he'd asked.

"Nothing at all, Mr. Logan. As long as she cooperates with our man and does what he says, she has nothing to worry about."

Marshall Logan could not get the words out of his head. *Does what he says?*

There was a first time for everything, but Marshall wasn't willing to bet that this was that time.

"Be careful," Joan called to him as he rushed out of the office. "And pick up some sun block."

TWELVE

Climbing out of the Datsun, Petra felt distanced from the things around her. As if watching someone else put bare feet down over cool, dark dirt. Disconnected. That was it. She felt disconnected. Separated. An observer of her own life.

It didn't work this way. Not if she wanted to stay in control.

Control? When had she been in control?

"Well," Vondel said, his sudden closeness startling her, "here we are. It's quiet here. Out of the way. You can rest."

Rest. Oh, yes, she could rest.

She noted the amenities that broke up the secluded beach. A fire pit, an adequate supply of dry wood, a small half tent. He'd been here before. "What's in there?" she asked, pointing to the lean-to.

"Drinking water, chairs. A change of clothes." He smiled. "Just the essentials."

Turning, she noticed the hammock strung between sturdy palms.

Vondel steered her towards it, his hand at the small of her back. "I think you will find it comfortable."

"Oh, I don't know," she said, looking at the simple twine bed in a whole new light, her senses flooding back to her, anxiety in the lead. "I — I haven't been in one of these since I was a kid."

"They haven't changed."

"Maybe not, but I have."

His look was deep. Engaging. It did not match his playful words. "Not much, I think." He helped ease her into the hammock over her protests. "I'll be here. With you. Please, Miss Logan, get some rest."

Suspended. Weightless.

Protected.

Too good to be true, Petra thought wearily, closing her eyes.

***

Frans spread the threadbare blanket over her, thoroughly aware of the shape it took on. He could easily tell where each piece of the pretty puzzle began. Where each ended. Long, smooth legs merged into the full, rich curves of her torso, her delicate arms and hands outlined by the light cover which absorbed each rise of her breast. Each breath.

How many hours had he spent watching her sleep? he wondered, then dismissed the question. How ever many it had been, how ever many more were to come, he sensed he would never tire of it. A small smile played with his mouth. As captivating as Petra Logan was roused, her down time always brought an odd comfort. The calm before the storm. Wherever she was now, in her dreams, it had to be less chaotic than Sava.

The soft breeze played with a loose, wavy tress before laying it over her lips. Frans reached down and brushed it gently away, the tips of his fingers hesitating before leaving the soft skin. He considered the last time she'd lain this close to him and stepped back as if to gain perspective. He'd never been an impulsive man, but this woman, Petra Logan, was making him one.

Frans tore his eyes away and looked out over the beach. It was a desolate, secluded place and, perhaps, he thought, the most beautiful he'd ever seen — the way the turquoise water played with the sand, bringing out its luster; the way it teased the sun, stealing some of its brilliance. This was his place. He'd discovered it shortly after arriving and had claimed it almost immediately, setting up his poor man's resort. It was where he came when he needed to get away. Regroup.

He'd been here two days ago when they first realized Trumad wasn't going to show. He'd spent the night in the lean-to, reliving every moment of the operation since Martin's arrival on Sava with Petra Logan, trying to figure out where they'd gone wrong. Where *he'd* gone wrong.

His operation. His failure. Five years of chasing the elusive, international crime lord who hid behind disguises and aliases so convincing no one had been able to identify him, had made the chase personal. It had not alarmed, or even occurred, to him until now that things had gone too far. That this business of cops and robbers had eclipsed everything else in his life.

Walking towards shore, he glanced over his shoulder to Petra. Her face was tilted in his direction. He couldn't make out her features from this distance, not clearly, but his last impression of her was still vivid.

How vivid would it have been if she'd succumbed to the dangers that had plagued her since her detainment? If he'd been too late to save her from the thugs who'd grabbed her or unable to fish her from the water?

Frans unfolded a worn lawn chair and sat outside the lean-to, the shade its shadow provided knocking some of the fire out of the air. He'd never been so sure about anything as he'd been about detaining her. It had seemed as natural as breathing. A stroke of luck. A much needed stoke of luck.

For years Frans and his team of agents had been chasing Trumad around the globe. The elusive crime king who'd spawned his legacy in the Netherlands and then smeared it throughout Europe and beyond was wanted in so many countries, he was almost legendary.

No one seemed to have a nose for Trumad like Frans. He always seemed to be just a step behind and most member countries of Interpol welcomed his leadership in the investigation, an investigation which eventually led to the Caribbean, where they suspected Trumad's dirty money was being dropped off and then shipped to North America.

After exhausting the other islands in lengthy undercover investigations, Sava, an island so small it had only one hotel, was investigated almost as a mere formality.

Although this absence of commercialization seemed to be what gave Sava its charm and attracted only the very elite, most of whom were content to sleep on whatever sea vessel had brought them to the island, as though they were roughing-it in the wilds, it seemed too unlikely, too open a spot for Trumad to conduct business.

However, soon after arriving, posing as a tourist, Frans was in the company of the chatty hotel owner, who, under the guise of gossip, confided that the island was not the peaceful little haven it seemed. They had, she'd assured him with a flirty wink, their share of excitement.

"Dey come wid da money, ya know," she'd said conspiratorially, leaning across the counter. "Big, shiny suitcases. Full to da top. Don' put in me safe." She'd rolled her eyes. "Keep it in de room. Unda' de bed."

Frans didn't ask, nor did he care, what Marta was doing under the beds, looking through the shiny cases they'd declined to keep in the hotel's safe. He believed her. The money was coming through Sava.

A closer look at the little community only con-
firmed this. With its assorted characters and colorful
pastimes, and with its shady history of having once
been a favorite haven for pirates, nobody was going to
make much over men with shiny suitcases on Sava.

The timing couldn't have been more perfect if
they'd planned it. Sava's Burgomaster at that time had
been begging Dutch authorities for a new assignment,
feeling he'd more than paid his dues.

Since the appointment of Burgomaster was per-
ceived by most Dutch law-enforcement professionals
as some kind of demotion or disciplinary action, Frans
saw replacing the Burgomaster as the perfect cover —
a washed-up cop with no ambition, whiling away his
days on an overgrown sandbar. Dutch authorities
agreed, and a couple of weeks later, Frans and a half-
dozen agents had relocated to the tiny island, planning
an interference that might lead them to the crime lord.
A waiting game, mostly, that had netted them little.

Until Petra Logan.

Back in Minnesota, at MidWest State Banks, she
had no idea what she'd stumbled upon. Then or now.
Martin had been careless. Red flags had gone up
everywhere and Martin's every breath had been
monitored since. The forensic banking department of
MidWest State Banks had fully cooperated with several
levels of government and law-enforcement agencies to
keep the investigation completely under wraps. Even
Marshall Logan had been kept in the dark, until now.

The discovery of Martin's skimming had made
some sense of the past two days. Trumad had never
showed because he'd never planned to. His only intent
had been to lure Clark to the Caribbean where he and
Petra would both be killed.

Having discovered the skimming, the authorities
were now moving in to try and chase down the rest of
Trumad's money before he pulled it all out and moved

it elsewhere without a trace. They had not yet identified all of the bogus accounts and no doubt Trumad had already begun to drain many of them. Following Trumad's money would be their only link to him should Petra Logan's detainment on Sava, exceptional bait as that was, fail to flush him out. Had Frans not nabbed her, the whole operation would have been blown out of the water since his team would have had no choice but to intervene on the *Surf Queen* in order to prevent her death. They had a couple of agents on board all along, but the most they could have hoped for in that situation would have been nabbing the hit man and arresting Clark Martin. At that point, Trumad would have had no choice but to cut his losses and be content with whatever money he'd been able to safely funnel elsewhere, and once again, maybe forever, Trumad would have eluded them.

He smiled thinly, remembering the way Petra had barreled up in the car, fire on wheels. The guilt he was feeling over having detained her was uncharacteristic, but deserved, he knew. He'd been saving her life, but that was only half true. He'd been using her too.

***

Clark was not in the mood for the Hardy Boys. They were cramping his style and, he suspected, up to something. Twice he'd asked them to get him a separate vehicle, something less conspicuous than that eyesore on wheels they traveled in, and twice they'd made excuses. Lame, pathetic excuses for excuses. Clark wasn't buying any of it. He'd been around, he knew the score. Bernard and Alphonse were deliberately getting their brainless, beefy selves between Clark and his duty. His saving grace. The one thing he could do to redeem himself to Trumad and regain standing. They were nasty, spiteful dolts who were making his life hell and Clark was simply not going to stand for it. Let them play with each other, he thought haughtily, he had bigger fish to fry.

Clark peered out the roadside window, catching a glimpse of the rust bucket and its hefty occupants adjacent to the hotel's parking lot and not, unbeknownst to them, particularly well hidden behind a thin row of palms. What kind of a joke was this?

"A sad one."

Damn, he did it again. His own voice answering his own question. Out loud. This had to stop.

It wouldn't take a whole lot of maneuvering to slip away from his *tail*. All he needed was a car and a head start.

Clark slapped on a tasteful helping of his favorite cologne and surveyed his reflection in the bathroom mirror. The tan he'd grown into over this otherwise disastrous vacation gave him a healthy, youthful glow and made the bleaching sessions with his dentist worth every cent. He looked, Clark thought, tipping his head side to side, catching his chiseled jaw line in the best light, European. Dignified. Debonair.

And if there was one thing about the little hotel that stood out to Clark as a true positive, it was the fact that it was run by women, the one thing Clark knew better than banking.

Another quick glance out the window assured Clark that Sherlock and Watson were still unwittingly stationed outside the hotel. It would have, of course, made sense for one of them to watch the back and one the front, but their blunders were his ticket to an easy getaway.

Now, about that car ...

***

Alexander's conversation with Bernard had been

not only excruciating, but disturbing. The information the brawny islander had offered suggested that Clark Martin had deliberately ignored his instructions to reconcile with Petra Logan and resume their trip to Barbados. The fact that the original plan had to be tinkered with a bit and Alexander's business with the duo delayed, was infuriating on its own. In fact, in all his dealings, Alexander had never been stood up or attached to such a bungled crusade as this. Yes, that had been a hard bullet to bite but he had. Calmly. Sensibly. All Martin had to do was get her back on the boat, and things would take care of themselves. The fact that Martin had no clue that his death was as impending as his fiancée's, just delayed a day in the original blueprint, worked well in managing the smug banker. Or, so he'd thought. This new set of circumstances had proved disastrous, and now Trumad felt the first pangs of a feeling so foreign, he'd only deciphered it by way of logic.

Panic.

He'd named it officially when he'd realized he could not reach Martin. Directly. His phone was either out of commission or disarmed. Either way, anger had burned its way through to torment, and these were feelings associated, he knew, with a weaker specimen. Alexander Trumad was a name that instilled fear and order. A strong name. A hard name. He could not expect Bernard and Alphonse, two beefy locals who pledged loyalty for a new set of tires and a hundred dollars a piece, to handle something with the danger potential of this. Another bullet to bite. He'd hired them to do the simplest of jobs — keep an eye on Martin and Logan and let him know if anything went wrong. That was it. How more clear could it be? Their sheer stupidity was supposed to make them unlikely suspects should anyone guess that he had any hired hands on Sava at this most delicate of times.

Never in his wildest dreams had he imagined that something so simple could go so wrong. Horribly wrong. If Martin bungled again, or even succeeded, and the authorities caught on, he would, no doubt, put the whole operation in jeopardy. There was not enough time to move all his money, without a trace, if Martin talked. Alexander could cut himself loose, of course, and let Martin babble on about their dealings, knowing full well they would never connect him, physically, to any crime, a benefit of being an unidentified crime boss. He could sail away, assuming the jet-set playboy persona he wore so well.

He could, but he wouldn't.

It was too much money. It was *his* money. Both those things outranked *cut-and-run* hands down.

He had to do it. There was really no other choice. He had to go to Sava and take care of Martin and Logan himself. It had become too risky relying on others. How did that old adage go?

If you want it done right, do it yourself.

Alexander wanted it done.

Right.

***

Marshall didn't bother trying to sleep during the four-hour flight to Caracas, reasoning he'd have time to rest at the hotel during his layover before catching the short late-morning cruise to Sava.

Marshall smiled at the little girl across the aisle, a tow-headed toddler with pink cowboy boots and a green plastic case opened to display the tools of her trade: Coloring Crayons, nibbled and peeled to stubs; plastic scissors, and a coloring book with action figures he did not recognize on the cover.

It had been a while. The years had run away from

him like wind off the lake; he couldn't deny the calender or the grey he had in what was left of his hair, but he could skip backward in a heartbeat. Back to the times he and his daughter traveled together, Joan in tow to keep an eye on the precocious Petra while Marshall attended meetings. Petra wasn't even three when her mother had passed away.

Petra was sweet and caring but she was also stubborn, willful and just this side of rebellious. If she believed she was right, then it only reasoned that she was, and she would exhaust any resource available to prove this to her father, wearing him down to reluctant agreement. It occurred to Marshall, twenty-thousand-feet over the plains of the Mid-West, that this was the one defining trait to last his daughter over three decades.

He had been a protective father, maybe even indulgent. Too indulgent? Every time he'd looked into his daughter's eyes, he'd seen her mother and couldn't find the words to say *no*. At least not often enough. Was it this lack of borders, boundaries that had made her so ... what, unsettled? He hadn't seen anything wrong in giving her every opportunity and desire of her heart. Yet, she wasn't spoiled in the way people think of spoiled.

The true problem, Marshall expected, was that his daughter was deeper than most and looking for something most wouldn't even know they were missing. His forehead creased with worry. Would she ever find it? When he'd finally clamped down and insisted she work for him, he had hoped it would give her some kind of purpose, direction, not lead to a deadly entanglement with the crime world. Was it too late to untangle her now?

... as long as she cooperates ...

... listens and does what he says ...

Marshall Logan could not get the words out of his head.

***

"Pure gold," Clark said with such fullness, such reflection, he could actually feel his chest swell. "Hate to part with it but, well, you being a business woman and all, I can hardly expect you to extend me any more favors without some kind of collateral."

The woman held the watch in her hands as if it were a living, breathing heart. Well, in a way, it was. Twenty-five-hundred-dollar time pieces didn't come the way of the common man.

"Rolex," Clark said. Say no more. Some things were universal. Elvis. *Rolex*.

"Ah, Rol-ex," repeated the woman with her island twang. Her phony savvy jabbed at his funny bone but he refused even a smirk. Business was, after all, business.

"I am looking for my — my ..." He'd done this before, rather well, he mused, and could do it again. "The woman I intend to marry." Clark felt wetness on the rims of his lids and carried on. "I know she's on the island, I just don't know where. I need to find her. I — I —"

Time for a mini breakdown. Women *loved* this stuff. Couldn't get enough of it.

He had contact and waited a long, laborious moment before looking up to acknowledge a stubby-fingered hand folded over his own. Perfect.

"Is there," he looked up, searching the round female face, "something I could get around in? A car, maybe? I'm in a pretty tough spot here."

He held her gaze. Hard. If she looked away, she would be lying. He didn't think she was a liar.

"A car?"

"Yes. Anything. I just —" He couldn't know which way she was leaning (he could guess, but the way things were going, certainty was desirable) "I need to find her. There are so few things in life that are certain but she — she," gulp, hold it, deep, deep breath, "she's the one for me. I have to find her. I just have to."

"Well, dere *is* someting ..."

Now, she was talking.

"I'm not picky."

Normal circumstances did not apply.

THIRTEEN

Frans peered towards the sun at his back, its journey down the horizon nearing completion as it continued to sweep long golden fingers everywhere. He wondered if Petra was still sleeping and walked over to where she lay suspended between the two trees, shadows, amidst ribbons of light, caressing her body in the gentle wind.

***

She'd been awake for some time, too content in the swinging bed to vacate its gentle arms, the horrors of the past two days seeming to have evaporated in the sun. She'd heard his soft approach, felt his shadow fall across her body. She knew, without seeing, that his face was bent over hers. A perfect moment that she didn't want to spoil with something so indifferent as ... reality. Her hair, she could feel, was almost dry. Her dress too. Warm. Snug. Safe. The only better place she could be was in his arms.

Without opening her eyes, she smiled and sighed. "Ah, this is the life."

She heard his chuckle, his breath soft on her cheek. Her eyes flew open; she'd known he was directly over her, but she hadn't realized how directly. Or how close. A blond fringe fell forward, over his cheeks and forehead, taking off a good twenty years. He must have been a cute boy. Dimples, blond curls and a grin as big as all outdoors. He'd probably had all the little girls' hearts on strings. Hers, apparently, was no exception. Could he hear the noisy heart and racing pulse that pounded in her own ears?

"You slept?"

It was impossible to ignore the electrical current his intense gaze sent through her body. She wanted to, but, well, it was like putting out a forest fire with a bucket of water.

"Yes, this hammock is wonderful. You should try it."

He smiled. Slow. Deliberate. "Is that an invitation?"

"Oh," she said, realizing what she'd just walked into. "I mean, what I meant was ..."

"Miss Logan." Still smiling, he squatted down next to the hammock; they were chin to chin. "I'd be most happy to accept your offer, but I'm still on duty for a few more hours."

"I wasn't — I was ..."

"Offering your affections?"

"Exactly!"

"Exactly?" A crease crinkled his brow. "I'm confused, Miss Logan. *Were* you offering or weren't you offering?"

"Oh, for the love of ..." How had she gotten this mess rolling? She sat up, intending to escape the hammock and Frans's intense grin.

It was a slow move, for what probably amounted to a split second, but before she could take a worried breath, the stretched twine and canvas contraption lurched, taking her with it.

It was his chest she fell into. A hard wide surface that smelled like skin, his skin, through the rugged khaki shirt. She pressed her face and fingers into it. His arms enfolded her. It felt better than she'd dreamed ... remembered.

She wanted more. As much as she could reach and

touch and hold. Hands moved up her back and into her hair. His breath was hot on her neck, his bristled chin moving over her, his lips brushing her ear and cheek. She turned her face, anticipating the crushing of his mouth. His face tightened as, instead of kissing her, he pulled her up in his arms and stood.

He carried her across the sand as if she were a child, his touch void of desire, his face no longer boyish or playful but purposeful. Had she imagined the way he'd held her back there?

No, there had been something. He'd felt it too, she was sure. He'd been just as reckless, just as hungry as she. What had happened? What had she done?

"I can walk," she said, the words sounding as cold as they felt.

"I've no doubts," he answered seriously, "but you know what they say."

"No, Burgomaster, what do they say?" She was watching the campsite over his shoulder as it shrank with distance. It occurred to her rather suddenly that they were headed in the wrong direction. That they were ... she twisted around to confirm her suspicions. Not only were they headed towards the water, they were nearly in it. She could almost feel the cool, moist influence of her dreaded foe.

"You can lead a horse to water," Vondel said, wading in, "and maybe, with a little luck, you can teach it a thing or two."

***

It looked empty. Dark.

The car was gone.

Clark tried parking the sputtering scooter on a flat stretch of earth behind the station, but the kick-stand tore away and it rolled on its side like a sick puppy. He glared, willing it a quiet death.

He'd look around. Why not? It was public property.

As Clark clung to the side of the rough brick building, edging his way to the front and, from what he could tell, only entrance, he realized he was alone. Totally alone. Not only were there no cars parked around the municipal structure, there were no cars anywhere. And he hadn't met or passed a single one on his way here. He stepped away from the building and shrugged into his normal, perfect posture. This sneaking around like a spy was not something he planned on becoming accustomed to. It seemed beneath him. He walked to the front of the building and let himself in like the man he was.

***

"Are you out of your mind?" Petra sputtered.

His arms remained strong. Resolved. He was holding her above the water. He said nothing.

"This isn't funny, Vondel," she warned, though it came out sounding like a plea. "Take me in."

"You don't swim." It was a statement, not a question. An icy fingertip ran down her spine. Was it a threat? Had the little voice she'd shut out been valid in suspecting the Burgomaster? It didn't seem possible; he'd been so — so, well, friendly. More than friendly. Maybe that was the way he worked. Instead of dragging her out kicking and screaming, he'd merely scooped her up in his arms and carried her out. She'd have gone with him anywhere. Could she have been that far off the mark?

"I do," she lied. "A little."

He seemed genuinely pleased with this information, and Petra relaxed a little in his arms. He could hardly be thrilled about this if he was planning on drowning her.

"How little?"

"Oh, you know." She let go of his neck with one hand and waved distractedly. "I'm not up for the next Olympics, or anything, but I do okay. As long as I'm not being shoved off a pier."

"Mmm-hm."

He didn't seem convinced. New tactic. "Let's go back and you can have the hammock, and I'll — I'll look around your little hideaway." She looked up hopefully. He didn't answer.

"No!" she gasped, the certainty of water hitting her like a ton of bricks. Cold, wet bricks. "You didn't mean —" Of course he had. She nervously shifted in his arms, trying to distance herself an inch or two from his intent. "I — I can't. I just can't, Vondel. You were right, I don't swim. Not a stroke!"

"This is an island," he said, looking directly into her eyes, "surrounded by water. Swimming comes in handy."

***

Her body quivered, her hands tightening around his neck as her lower limbs broke the surface. "I'm going to set you down slowly," Frans breathed into her ear. "You can stand. It's not deep."

"I —" She searched anxiously for the bottom with an outstretched foot. "I don't think this is such a great idea."

Settled now on both feet, her stance, what was visible above the water line that marked her dress just below the swell of her breasts, appeared less than firm. She held his hands, both of them, keeping the physical contact between them continuous, as good an indication of her fear as the trembling of her body.

"I don't have a suit, remember?" she continued, trying to make light of the situation. "We could go back and look for one in that little shop —"

"You didn't have a suit on when you went off the pier." He moved a small step back. Away. Let his fingers loosen on his end of the grip.

"Well, no," she covered the step he took and added another for good measure, "but that was an unusual situation."

She was beautiful in this half light. Amber bars reached out from the melting sun, sprinkling golden highlights on the contours of a full mouth and wide-set eyes. Her hair, reflecting the fire-lit sun, became the color where it met the water. Her quick, shallow breaths drew his eyes to the quivering hollow just above that incredible little dress he knew would cling even more deliciously to her wet than it had dry.

He wanted to wrap this scared creature up in his arms more than he could ever remember wanting anything. He almost did. Almost.

She had to save herself. It was the thing that defined her. The thing that pulled him to her so very hard. And the thing that pushed him away. Petra Logan was struggling to stay on top. If she began to rely on him, if he allowed her to, she would leave Sava a different woman than the one who'd crashed into his life and turned it upside down. He couldn't let that happen. She was perfect just the way she was.

"I'm going to let go," he cautioned, his fingers straightening and slipping from hers.

"No!"

He watched her try to pull back her reaction with a calmer version. "It's getting dark. I — I won't be able to see you."

"The moon," he replied. In minutes a large, three-quarter moon, would shower them with light.

"Don't leave me, Vondel," she demanded.

"I'm not going anywhere," he answered over the few feet of water that separated them before giving her a wide grin. "I'm still waiting for you to answer my question." He could make out her shape but details were dependent on memory. He had a few reams rolling around in his head.

"Question?"

"Surely you remember our little, uh," he cleared his throat for effect, "conversation." She was already forgetting the water. "Were you or were you not offering me ..."

Water splayed over his chest and shoulders. Frans threw his head back and laughed. "I take that to mean the offer has been rescinded."

"Take it anyway you want, Burgomaster."

***

Marta held the watch out and glared with disgust. Already the gold plating was chipped from the face. She didn't need her jeweler's glass to determine the authenticity of the *diamond* that marked twelve.

Rolex? Huh! It wasn't even one of the better imitations she'd seen. This Martin fellow was one of a kind. The kind that should go as far away from Sava, and her, as he could get. After all, he'd humiliated that poor woman he'd been with, loud enough for the entire staff, not to mention their traveling companions, to hear. Marta had heard a squabble or two in her day, especially since taking over the little hotel, but the things he said to his fiancée that night, well, they made her blush. She couldn't claim to be an authority on romance but she doubted seriously that Miss Logan's disinterest in intimacy with the slick, cocky American had as much to with her as it did with him.

She was a beauty, Marta thought. Not blonde and overly tanned like the women who usually traveled with Martin's type, but striking in a way Marta doubted he could even comprehend.

Frans could. He'd been more wrapped up in the

woman than anything else she'd seen since his arrival as Sava's new Burgomaster several months back.

Sava, though subject to much of the same criminal code as the Netherlands, tended to think and act like it were self-governed, and with respect to its own matters it was. Savans ran Sava and created and implemented its own by-laws; the Burgomaster enforced both the criminal and civic laws, appointed and called upon deputies when needed, and served as a vehicle through which more complicated matters were passed on to higher governing bodies to settle. Were Sava not so puny and its way of life not so simple, the position of Burgomaster, a quasi mayor, chief of police and civic clerk all rolled into one, might be considered a prestigious position.

Not that Savans deemed the position as without honor. On the contrary. Sava might be the butt of jokes in the Caribbean, but Savans were fiercely proud of their tiny haven and did their best to win over their Burgomasters and usually succeeded. Not that any Burgomaster had ever stayed longer than he had to, but at least when he left, Sava was esteemed in his eyes. There was, of course, the odd exception, like the last Burgomaster. A miserable man the island couldn't wait to be rid of and had no trouble showing it.

Such a contrast to Frans. The very handsome Burgomaster was by far the most liked that Marta could remember — a man's man, the kind of man every man wanted to be and every woman wanted. Yes, the delicious Frans was the undisputed champion of gossip among the locals. Why had such an eligible man, one so obviously educated and charismatic, come to Sava? And why did he seem to have no ambition to leave, no interest in furthering his career?

As odd as it seemed, it did not derail mothers from pushing their daughters in his direction. It did not, in some cases, derail mothers from pushing themselves in his direction. Since his arrival, Frans had been gallantly fending off the attentions of a good portion of Sava's female population.

He was safe with Marta. She was content with the fact that she was too old and too busy to chase after a husband or a lover. Their first encounter had been a friendly one, putting Frans immediately at ease. She'd assumed he was just a tourist, but when he showed up again a few weeks later as the new Burgomaster, she realized he'd been checking out the place that was going to be his home for the next couple of years.

There was something more going on with Frans, though. Something that extended beyond the position of Burgomaster. She'd sensed this from the start, but she also knew that whatever it was he could not tell her. Not yet. She hadn't pressed. Clark Martin was involved. Somehow. And so was Miss Logan. She'd bet her life on it.

***

"I can't swim in this dress," she complained, still looking for an escape from the water.

"You should take it off then," he suggested, giving her something he thought might pass for a leer.

"Nice try, Vondel. By the way, where did you get this dress? You do seem to have a rather eclectic assortment of women's clothing stashed away at *headquarters*."

He laughed. "Oh, you know how it is, things just get left behind." Her face told him she was still more than a little curious. Jealous perhaps? It was something he'd enjoy pursuing the answer to later, when all of this was over. If she was still as interested. Things would change for them both when it was over.

"What are you doing?" she demanded, her voice coming out in a little squeak when he began to unbutton his shirt.

"Miss Logan, the first thing you should do is unveil yourself of restricting garments." He pulled it over his head. It was wet and heavy, which made it easy to cast ashore. He was glad to be rid of it. Besides, they were going out deeper soon.

She watched him wade further out, wordlessly crouching in the water a good twenty feet away. She had come so far, he thought, aware of the affection this realization produced. Her fear of the water was sincere, rooted more deeply than the accident this afternoon, he knew. Whatever it was, whatever had happened had to have been severe to instill such trepidation in a woman so full of fire and confidence.

"Petra," he said simply. She knew what he wanted her to do.

"It's a little chilly," she said, moving towards him, her full bottom lip trembling. It wasn't the temperature. It was now, seeing the trust in her eyes behind the fear, this single moment in the moonlit water, that he realized the depths of his feelings.

***

The phone startled Clark and he jumped. It was so quiet here, and he'd been so immersed in his task. It did not escape him, as he rummaged through closets and dresser drawers, that had Petra not refused him the other night, humiliating and infuriating him into losing his temper, he would be on Barbados now with Trumad, sipping Mai Tais and accepting praise for a job well done. And money. Lots and lots of fresh pressed currency. The kind you didn't feel responsible for reporting on the long form.

Instead, he was rooting around a musty old building on a throwback island whose inhabitants were, well, hardly the ilk of civilized society. Any qualms he had regarding Petra's *disappearance* had long since evaporated.

There was only one bed. He looked, he knew. Long strands of red hair glistened on the pillow case. She was sleeping with the cop. The cop! A man she hardly knew. A lowly civil servant content to pass his days chasing stray dogs *and* sleeping with *his* fiancée! The fiancée who, after a year of his doting attention, had the nerve to turn *him* away. Clark had this Caribbean Neanderthal beat hands down in every category imaginable and yet she chose *him*. Instead. To *sleep* with. Maybe that's where he'd gone wrong. Maybe all he'd needed was a badge to lure the icy Petra to his sheets.

It was too much. Clark wanted to wipe the slate in his mind clean so he could concentrate on, well, what exactly *was* he doing? Looking for a clue as to where she might be.

The phone was driving him nuts.

"Frans?"

Someone was here. Inside. With him.

He should hide.

A quick inspection of the room changed his mind. In his hurry, his anger, he'd pretty much torn the bedroom apart. That could be a problem.

Clark took a deep breath, straightened his shoulders and exited the bedroom, moving towards the sound of the voice.

"Frans?"

A kid, Clark discovered. Piece of cake.

"Doesn't look like anyone's here," he said in his friendliest tone. "I thought maybe someone was in the back, but it's empty."

"Oh," said the boy with disappointment. His brow was scrunched up like an old man's. "Who are you?"

He spoke English. This made things a *whole* lot

easier.

"Clark Martin," he said, extending his hand.

"I am Eric," the boy said with evident trepidation though he fit his slender hand into Clark's.

"Glad to meet you, Eric," Clark said, making full eye contact. "I'm looking for someone, and I was hoping the Burgomaster could help me out. You haven't seen a strange woman anywhere, have you? Tall? Lots of red hair?"

"N — no," said the boy, looking away.

Lying. The little snot was lying. He knew *exactly* whom Clark was talking about.

"Well," Clark engaged the boy's gaze again, and kept his words soft, though he wanted to turn him over his knee and spank the little jerk until he came clean, "I had to ask. She's my fiancée and I'm a little worried about her."

"Fiancée?" the boy asked, confusion contorting pointy, youthful features. "You mean like gettin' married?"

"Yes, Eric," Clark feigned a little laugh, "that's exactly what I mean."

"You don' know where she at?"

Suddenly, Clark didn't like the way this was going. "I'm going to hang around a little longer and see if anyone shows up," Clark said, dismissing the boy. "Is there a message I can give the Burgomaster for you?"

"No." The boy backed away towards the door. "No, message."

"Goodbye, Eric. It's been a pleasure."

***

Petra knew she was shaking, knew Frans could see it, though he said nothing. It wasn't like her to worry over what others thought, but she found herself increasingly interested in what was going on in

Vondel's head about her. Did he think it silly that a grown woman was afraid of the water? Amusing?

If so, it didn't come across. His efforts seemed sincere, though his methods were questionable. His carrying her out here the way he had, both of them clothed, seemed like something out of a movie. The strong, fearless man taking charge of the hapless, helpless little female. He didn't think her helpless, did he? Hapless, she could see in light of recent events, but helpless? Well, okay, maybe she could see that too, but really, she had an excuse, didn't she? Admittedly, the water thing was a drawback but ...

She could do this. He'd see.

***

This was a colossal waist of time, Clark thought with disgust.

Every minute he'd spent on this wretched island fell into that category.

He surveyed the room to make sure he'd put it back the way he'd found it. It looked good to him.

He had to get Petra. Alone.

The cop was a problem.

The boy had seemed like a problem, a very small, annoying problem, but Clark had knocked that one out of the ballpark.

Good thing the kid hadn't seen the gun.

Clark had never fired a gun before. He'd never even held one but, well, there it was. Anyone rummaging through the Burgomaster's quarters would have found it. How bright was that?

The cold steel, tucked efficiently (and quite professionally, Clark thought) into the waistband of his shorts made him feel invincible. Well, he was. Invincible. One, or two, little setbacks were hardly enough to put him out of the running.

He remembered the can of lighter fluid he'd seen next to what had seemed like some sort of primitive barbecue. There was more than one way of flushing Petra out, and this was as good a place as any to start.

FOURTEEN

"Excuse me?" Her voice cut over the still water to him. "I believe that was my breast."

Frans caught the laugh in his throat. "Excuse me," he answered dryly, "I didn't know."

"Right, Vondel," she said teasingly, pushing her body through the water and away from him.

"Twenty feet," he ordered, ignoring her insinuation.

"This is twenty feet."

"You stopped. I saw you."

"No."

"I know what I saw," he insisted.

"I know what I felt."

This time he did laugh. "You are flattering yourself, Miss Logan. I am merely trying to instruct you."

"Well, I'm coming back now, so why don't you try instructing me with your hands in plain sight."

Frans held his arms above the water and then rested them on the surface. "As you wish."

He watched the bobbing head and hint of body steal through the water smoothly. Her progress was astounding and alluded that she had, at some point in her life, actually enjoyed the water. She arrived in front of him, ceremoniously bouncing. He'd carefully maneuvered them out a bit deeper each lap. If she'd noticed, she hadn't mentioned it.

"See how powerful you are? How clean you cut the

water? You're a natural."

Her dress sagged a little with the weight of water, and the three-quarter moon sparkled down her front as if its only intent was to spotlight the crevasse between her high, firm breasts.

She nodded to his words, then submerged herself neck-deep into water. Her reaction to his? He grinned. Did she have even an inkling of the things he thought looking at her and envying the water's freedom to touch every part of her?

"I think I've got the hang of this floating stuff," she interjected, taking control of the uneasy silence. "What's next? Shouldn't I be kicking up a lot of water and twirling my arms over my head. Oh, I know!" she said. "How about the breast stroke? I bet you're an expert at that one."

Frans let out a loud laugh. "I haven't had any complaints until now."

"There's always a first time for everything, Vondel."

"Good, then that means you are ready to tread water."

***

"Tread water?"

"We're going to move out a little," he said, putting his hands around her waist.

She didn't pull away. "How much is a little?"

"Don't worry, you're doing fine."

"I'm not worried," she said, fending off his concern, though worry washed lightly over her words. "I — I can do it myself."

"Petra, there's a dip —"

"Augh!" she screamed, finding it on her own. She bobbed uneasily until she was able to grab onto him. "This isn't funny, Vondel."

"Frans," he said simply, his hands finding her waist

again. Well, okay, they tended to find a little more than her waist, but she was secure and had to confess, not to him of course, that she really didn't mind.

"It's not so deep." He was still standing head and shoulders above the water.

"I can't touch!"

"Sh-h-h," he cooed, "you'll wake up the sharks."

"I'm going in now," she said, searching frantically for the beach over his shoulders but making no move to let go. "I'm going in now," she repeated. "It's too deep."

***

"If someone shoves you off a pier again," he said, making the argument, though he knew it would not happen again, not on his watch, "you can bet it will be into water deeper than this."

"Let me go!" she said angrily, ignoring the sense of his words.

"I'm trying to help you, Petra," he said. "I don't take my responsibilities lightly."

She was clinging to him and trembling, but her fight was only in her words. "Don't let go of me yet."

Frans spread his fingers so his hold on her would seem bigger. Sturdier. "I won't," he assured. "When you're ready."

"Tell me what to do, but don't let go of me."

"A reasonable request."

"Don't try getting on my good side, Vondel. You're in deep enough."

"Frans," he corrected.

"Frans."

"So, are you," he said, crouching in the water so they were eye level.

She finally broke the gaze. "This treading water thing, does it always work?"

"If done correctly."

"I'll float?"

"With some effort, yes."

"I won't sink?"

"I would not let that happen."

"How?" The word was barely out when panic seized her. "Don't show me, just tell me. I need you ..."

"About time you figured that out."

She pulled back a full arm's length, though still attached, and looked squarely at him. "You know what I mean. I need you to hold me up until I get this thing down."

"My pleasure."

"No doubt."

Frans threw back his head and laughed heartily. How long since he'd laughed this way? "It's very easy. Really. You have arms and legs. Both strong. The arms move across the water like this." He freed an arm from her waist to demonstrate the movement. She flinched with the change in support but didn't take her eyes off him. "Almost but not quite on top of the water. Back and forth. Easy."

"It seems slow," she challenged. "Won't I go under? Won't I need more momentum to stay afloat?"

"Perceptive," Frans teased. "I like that in a woman. That's where your legs come in. You kick them at the same pace. Back and forth through the water. Like scissors. Too fast and you'll tire quickly; too slow and you'll —"

"Sink?"

Frans ignored the fearful interruption. "Resistance is what you're after. And rhythm. The greater the resistance, the smaller and slower the movements. This is what you want. Small movements use less energy. Ideally, you should be able to carry on a conversation and keep afloat. The rhythm, once you find it, will help."

"I'm not sure I understand."

She looked like she understood.

"I can talk all night, but you will understand better once you try it."

"No, please. Not yet," she pleaded. "I'm not ready. Tell me again."

Frans remained firm. "Resistance. Arms across. Rhythm. Legs back and forth. There is little else to say."

She inhaled deeply. Once. Again. "You'll grab me if I — I go down?"

Frans nodded. "As always, my pleasure."

She let go.

Her first attempt, Frans noted, echoed what he'd witnessed earlier at the pier. Her arms flailing chaotically, no undercurrent from her legs. He reached out and grabbed her clumsily before her head went under.

"Its not working!" she snapped.

"You need to breathe," Frans offered. "Your lungs have to be full of air. When you panic you lose air. Air is lighter than —"

"Mass. I've taken physics, too, thank you very much. Sounds like a load of crap to me."

Her eyes trapped moonlight and looked to Frans more challenged than angry. He laughed. "Again. This time with more —"

"Air?" she finished. "And, incidentally, Frans, you grabbed my breast again. Don't think I'm not onto you."

He smiled but played it straight. "If so, it was not my intent. Perhaps if they were more ... prominent."

"I'd float better and wouldn't need you. More air."

She seemed more relaxed now in spite of her failed attempt.

"Here goes."

She pushed away from him and, as in her last effort, flailed. Frans was just about to reach for her when he felt movement. Under the water.

Her legs. She'd found her legs. He watched her head bob, her face strewn in concentration. It could go either way. Her shoulders slipped under, the water crested her chin. Then, she was up. Her motions slowed to a pace. A rhythm.

"Good! Very good! How does it feel?"

"Okay, I guess." She glanced up at him then back to her arms. They moved slow and steady in wide strokes.

"How long do I do this?"

"As long as you need to."

"Meaning?" She threw him a demanding look.

"Well, people have been known to tread water for days."

"Fascinating. Now really, Frans, I think I've got the hang of it. Come and get me."

Frans skimmed past her in the water.

"Hey, what's going on?" She turned towards him. "Frans, come and get me."

"Don't use up all your energy on needless excitement."

"Needless — oh, Frans, I —"

"You should be able to carry on a conversation. It's important you don't become breathless."

"It's important you get me out of here," she countered.

"You can get yourself out," he said, knowing the effect this judgment would have on her. "There's a sandbar here. You can make it this far."

"Thanks for the vote of confidence," she said warily.

"I'll make you a deal. If you can make it over here, and I know you can, I will tell you something. Something you'll be interested in."

"About that box in your closet?"

***

He started with the bed. It was the logical choice. It would soak up the lighter fluid and go up like a torch. In a way, it, the bed, was a symbolic gesture meant to avenge his ego. From the bed, he poured a trail leading up to the door, dousing it and the chair in one swift squeeze. He dropped the empty can ceremoniously and pulled out the match.

There was that moment. The moment in which an explosion gathers up its ignition, giving no hint that it's accepted it, no hint of what's to follow. Clark knew about the moment and stepped away, towards the window. It was a good thing.

The flames jumped straight up off the little bed, accompanied by thick, black smoke. The ceiling above it turned brown, instantly, the paint already cracking and peeling. The line of lighter fluid he'd traced to the bathroom door and chair hosted a running blue flame that multiplied a hundred fold as it reached its destination.

"Gotta go," he said, heading for the window. Damn, there was that voice again! His.

The smoke was getting thicker. He yanked on the window ledge, expecting a blast of fresh air that would set the whole place off like a Roman Candle.

It didn't budge.

He hadn't thought to check the window first.

"Swift, Martin." Oh, everybody's a critic, even his own voice!

He turned back to examine his handy work. He'd done well. So well, there was no chance of getting past the bed to the office. And the front door. The only door.

He tried the window again. Maybe it was just stuck. Or locked. There was nothing to pick up and force through the window and he was running out of time.

The gun. Of course. It was loaded; he'd at least had the forethought to check that. He'd just shoot his way out, like in the old days. Movies. Feeling rather heroic, Clark pulled the revolver free of his waistband and aimed.

***

"Wet sandy clothes," Petra complained when she trudged onto shore and out of the murky depths that no longer held such terror for her, not that she was in any rush to go back in. She could wait for that. A long time. "You sure know how to treat a girl to a good time, Frans."

"I have a few things here," he said, gesturing towards the lean-to she'd noticed on arrival.

"Another box? Is this a regular thing for you?"

"I usually come alone," he answered simply.

Usually. She felt her heart sink. He usually came alone. Why hadn't he said, always? *I always come alone*, was what she'd wanted to hear. *Until now. Until ... you.*

There she went again, reading more into things than was there. As if his life had started the day she arrived. As if hers had.

Frans brought over a couple of towels and a worn replica of the shirt he'd been wearing earlier. She patted the water from her arms and slipped into his shirt. Its arms hung down to her knees. It smelled like him. Musk and sea. She could feel his eyes on her as she slipped her arms up underneath and tugged the dress free, letting it fall to her feet.

"Your hair," he said, pulling a threadbare towel over her head, massaging it gently, each stroke a caress.

Her legs were rubber, her chest ready to explode

and her heart was up to a thousand beats a second.
She lifted her face.

Look at me.

His thumbs grazed behind her ears.

Look at me!

And then, he did.

He looked into her. Took her in, held her in his
eyes. His lips parted, his breath spilling out over her.
His fingers were on her neck, in her hair. His arms
pulled her into him, his mouth crushed down over
hers. She felt him with her hands and her mouth and
her skin. She pulled him to her. She wanted more.
Everything. Every part of her to touch every part of
him.

She could stay like this forever. This moment. This
place.

This man.

No one had ever kissed her this way. No one had
even come close.

"Petra," he murmured, his lips roughly grazing the
skin behind her ear.

She couldn't answer. Not with words. It would all
come back to her soon enough. Speech. Appetite. A
breathing pattern void of gasps. But for now ...

Who cared?

She rolled her head back, baring her neck. His lips
traced a line of fire from her ear to her collarbone.
Tender, lingering kisses. His hands scooped up her
back and pulled her up into him. Her legs were soft,
unsteady. She couldn't tell if she was holding up any of
her own weight. She wanted from Frans Vondel all the
things Clark could never give her. All the things she
could not give him, or anyone, until now.

Now, these thing controlled her. Pinned her against
him in a struggle she'd given up on when his eyes met
hers in the moonlight. Things so foreign, so wonder-

ful, they consumed her. Wholly. She never had a chance.

His mouth climbed the arch of her neck, finding hers again. Waiting. His hand at the back of her head was a gentle force. His kiss softened as his hands pulled on the collar of her shirt, his shirt, slipping it down her shoulders.

"Frans." She was breathless. Beyond breathless. "I, oh, I —"

"Petra," he whispered, his mouth sending tremors through her as they left a hot trail on her skin.

"It's just," she struggled. It had never, ever been like this before. She wanted him to know. Needed him to know. "I've never felt —"

"I know," he breathed into her neck.

I know.

What? What did he know?

No. No!

The fight. Had the whole island heard?

Petra pulled away, putting inches that seemed like miles between them. She couldn't speak the words. They were too horrible.

He tugged her playfully back towards him, but she resisted. "You are so beautiful," he said, that smile playing up in the shadows of his face. "Clark Martin is a fool."

He did know.

So, this was it. The game. The looks. The touching. He'd heard about her problems with Clark and while he had her here (she wasn't going anywhere for a couple of days anyway, right?) he'd taken it upon himself to cure her. Petra Logan, the last female frontier. To go where no man had gone before. At least, no man on this island, including the one she was supposed to be marrying. How could she have been so naive? Frans Vondel wasn't swept away by anything deeper than — than ego gratification.

"We have to get back," she said coolly, untangling the last of her now reclaimed limbs from his. "You said so yourself. You have things to do."

He looked genuinely confused but she wasn't falling for it. She'd fallen for this boyish, innocent act once too often and look where it had gotten her — alone on a deserted beach with the island rogue on the way to putting another notch on his belt. Another trophy for the box.

"Please," she said, pulling the oversized shirt back into place, wishing she could give it back. Right now, she didn't want anything from him except a wordless ride back to the station.

"If that's what you want."

"It is."

He looked at her oddly. She read disappointment and ... something else. She didn't know what it was but it didn't matter. He didn't try to dissuade her and she was glad, at least, for that.

He gathered up the towels and followed her to the car in steps so big they threatened to surpass hers. What would they say now? What was there to say? She dreaded the awkward silence that would swallow them up in the car.

"Petra," he said, once in the car, "I'm not sure what just happened back there but —"

"Nothing," she said adamantly. "Leave it at that."

"It seemed like something to me," he said, the moonlight casting shadows over his face.

Petra looked away, out the window, masking the effect he still had on her. She had to be stronger. Smarter.

Safe.

"I just went a little crazy," she said. "Don't worry, Burgomaster, it won't happen again." The words sounded so cold she hardly believed she'd said them to a man she'd been ready to ... She glanced over to find him staring over the steering wheel into the sea. He looked about a million miles away. Was a million miles far enough to keep her from making the same mistake twice? After this catastrophe, it didn't feel far enough.

FIFTEEN

He'd moved too fast. It was the only thing he could think of.

She'd been through so much in the past two days. Perhaps she'd become vulnerable to him. He'd seen it before in his line of work. Victims confusing gratitude with affection. Frans had always been careful to realign their emotions without shattering their pride. He had never taken advantage of them.

Never. Until now. But he hadn't read Petra like that. What he saw had seemed real. In fact, he was still sure it was. It was for him. Maybe for the first time. He'd never wanted any woman the way he wanted her. Had he tossed aside twenty years of experience trying to get her? Maybe this time, he was the one confusing something for love.

He looked over at the breathtaking woman curled up in his shirt in the seat beside him. No, he wasn't confused.

But he was, as he gazed into a sky burning brightly in the night, intrigued. Where the devil was the smoke coming from? He knew where it seemed to be coming from. He'd better call Rolphe and find out, once Petra was safely stowed away on the boat, the real headquarters, since it appeared the other one was in flames.

***

"A boat?" Petra asked incredulously, blowing her vow to stay calm, ignore him, or, if at all possible, both. She reached for his sleeve but missed it as he traveled in long, deliberate steps towards one of the piers she'd not yet been thrown off of. "You want me to stay on a boat? What's wrong with headquarters?"

"It's a nice boat," he said, disregarding her questions completely and offering her, instead, that smile. The big, Burgomaster smile that had undone her at least twice today. An infuriating smile. "It once belonged to a second cousin of Frank Sinatra."

"I don't care if it belonged to Elvis," she retorted, trying to catch up to him so he could see the look that went with the tone. Get the whole effect. "I'm not staying on it."

"No?" he said with a sidelong glance and a raised eyebrow.

"Not a chance."

"You are still under my jurisdiction, Petra," he said, his pace slowing as they neared the object of her complaint. "Or have you forgotten?"

Had she? For a moment? Back at that little hideaway he'd lured her away to, back when he'd folded her up in his arms and pushed his fingers into her hair, had she forgotten?

For a moment she had. She blushed remembering just how easily. The moonlight. The water. She wasn't about to let it happen again. "I haven't forgotten," she said, meeting his stare before walking past him to the plank.

***

The siren's wail began the precise moment the old, lumbering truck passed Clark. More than merely startled, he'd thought, for a fleeting second, that he was about to be arrested. So startled he lost controlling interest in the roughed-up scooter, allowing it to steer him off the road and into a sandy ditch.

The noise lessened with distance. They were not after him. They were after the fire he'd left burning.

Clark's attempts to drag the scooter back up to the road were futile. He left the miserable machine behind and climbed up to the road alone. Hitching a ride, he realized, in his smoky, disheveled clothes, was not an option. Nor could he return to the hotel like this either. Besides, that snot-nosed snit, Eric, would probably already be tattle-telling around the island. He had to clean up. Wash away the only evidence that could link him to the unfortunate accident at the police station. An accident he was sure would now give Petra no place to hide.

Clark all but stumbled onto the beach. Private. Secluded. Just what he was he looking for. A quick dip and he'd be ready to roll. He spied a tacky lean-to and moth-eaten hammock. A squatter's paradise, he sneered.

He could have kept his clothes on and washed them as he doused the smoke off his body, but he opted for separate rinse cycles. Apparently, so had somebody else.

Crumpled in the moonlight, sunken in the sand. Flowers. Yellow. Petra! He glowered around the beach. Nothing! Not even a ripple in the water. But soon. Very soon. This island was only so big. And he was just a step behind.

He lifted the dress, sand and water dripping from it. What was she wearing now? Likely that half-baked cop.

Disgusted by his own imagination, he flung the dress back to the sand and strolled into the water. Fifty feet from shore, the water was warm, shallow and still, only the occasional rustling of leaves interrupting the overwhelming sound of nothing. Silence.

And giggling.

Giggling?

Clark saw motion but could not detail it. Someone was on the shore. More, he thought, than one. Whispers. Petra and her cop? A crude whoop. More giggling.

No, kids. Just kids. Big deal. He'd scare them away like mice.

"Hey, you!" he called to figures he could, just now, make out. "Get out of here! Go home!"

More giggling. Then, no giggling. They'd left. As he'd known they would. His commanding presence and all.

No longer able to smell the smoke on himself, Clark pushed his naked frame forward and out of the water. Time to wash his clothes.

Gone! The dress too.

He dashed to the lean-to and poked his head inside. Nothing! Even if Petra and that jerk cop had left something behind, those little ... Clark scrambled up the slippery slopes, too livid to think. Those rotten, snotty-nosed little urchins! When he caught up with them, they were going to wish they'd never been born. He'd take them down a notch or two. He'd — he'd never see his clothes or the miserable little motor bike again!

There was no mistaking the sputter he'd come to hate. He made a dash towards the odd rhythmic grinding, coming just over the ridge of the ditch in time to see the blinking tail light bounce out of sight and into the unending darkness.

The gun. What about his gun?

He'd tossed it into the hammock after stripping. Had they seen it? Taken it?

Clark ambled, naked and irate, to the place he'd left it.

Let it be there, he thought.

The metal casing did not exactly glimmer in the moon's light, but it did reflect a muted sort of illumination. Clark snatched it up and pressed it into his side, forgetting, for the moment, that he had no waistband to tuck it into because he had no pants.

That was a problem, but somehow the gun made it seem less of one. He was no longer just a stranded, naked tourist. He was a stranded, naked tourist with a loaded gun. Big difference.

***

"Petra, would you like something to eat?" Frans asked.

She shrugged, her back to him as she gazed out over the water from the open back of the cruiser.

She hadn't said a word to him since climbing aboard. A shrug here, a nod there. She was not at all pleased about having to stay on the boat, but he'd realized, from the moment he'd seen her flailing in the water, that the station house was no more secure than the pier. The fire had proved that.

But the boat was only a small part of the fury in her eyes. The same fury she'd had when he'd first stopped her. Something had happened between them, back on the beach. Something more than a misunderstanding or an embarrassing moment.

He stood behind her a moment longer, mesmerized by the mantle of spun red silk spread across her supple back. He wanted to take her in his arms. Turn her around and pull that defiant little chin of hers up with his fingers, long enough for his mouth to find hers. Watch the lids of her velvety-blue eyes come halfway down as her body faltered against his.

Frans rubbed a hand over his face and backed away into the door of the cabin. "I'll be in here, if you need me."

"Fat chance."

Frans smiled. It wasn't much, but at least they were

talking.

***

"Bernard," Alexander bellowed into the receiver, "are you there? Can you hear me?"

There was a barrage of indescribable noise filling his ear, and Alexander held the little phone away before trying again.

"Bernard! Alphonse!" He was too irritated and too wired to hide his impatience any longer. Why should he? He was Alexander Trumad. The Alexander Trumad. The most demanding and least forgiving man on earth. Perhaps this did not translate accurately in ... Savan. "Answer me at once!"

"H'lo'... H'lo'. Anybody dere?"

Alexander massaged the vein on his forehead and took a deep breath. "This is Trumad."

"H'lo?"

The vein began to throb.

"This is Trumad!" he tried again. He heard a promising grunt.

"Meessar Trumad?"

"This is Trumad," he answered, every syllable a knife in his side. "Who am I speaking —"

"Trumad on de phone, Bernard. Wake up."

There could be an explanation, he told himself as the vein gravitated from throb to pump.

"It would be wise of the two of you to stay awake. I need Martin's position when I arrive."

"Po-zi-shun?"

"Yes, position. His location." Dead silence. "Where he is."

"Oh, yeah, yeah. We know where he at."

"Wonderful." Alexander's sarcasm was wasted on the pair, but he needed it for his own benefit. "Now, just keep him in your sights at all times."

"How 'bout when we sleep?"

No. He could not be hearing this.

"Take turns if you have to. I need Martin's —"

"Po-zi-shun!" One of them, Alphonse.

"Yes," Alexander answered, "very good. I can see you have everything under control there."

"We don' sleep no more."

We? Did he say we? Alexander wasn't sure he even wanted the answer. Surely, between the two enormous heads they had come to the conclusion that one of them needed to stay awake if the other one slept.

"I'll keep in touch," he said, folding up the phone and throwing it off the yacht.

***

She was hungry. Starving. She'd thought she'd be able to hold out a little longer, but the smell coming from inside the cabin undid her resolve. When had she last eaten? As if pushed along by invisible forces, Petra found herself entering the paneled cabin. It was nearly as dark inside as it was out, and she held back in the doorway.

"You will be joining me, Petra?"

She found his form in the darkness, a single, amber glow flickering between them. He looked enormous, his shadow climbing the wall behind him. His eyes picked up the meager light. Met hers.

"Do you always feed your prisoners by candlelight, Vondel?"

"It's a lantern," he said, directing her with a gesture that was illuminated in the shifting light. "But it is nice, don't you think? It seems harsh to light up the cabin when the water around it is so peaceful."

The effect was striking, she had to admit. The calm, dark water and skies swallowing them up but for this glimmer. It made her feel like whispering. As if the sound of their voices would break the lull open. With small steps she came towards him.

Frans jumped to his feet and to her side. "Let me help you," he said, guiding her to one side of an intimate booth. Settled back on his side, Petra was aware of just how intimate. Close. His wide shoulders seemed to loom over her in the glow of the lantern. She felt something under the table.

His knees.

A spark.

Petra pulled her legs back and avoided his eyes. "Bread and water?" she asked in a tone she tried to keep even.

"Perhaps next time, if you wish," Frans said, lifting the lid off a large metal pot, releasing an aroma she could recognize in her sleep. "This is a little island delicacy we like to call crab."

Seafood by candlelight.

A more naive woman might *think* the Burgomaster was trying to woo her into his arms ... into his bed.

Petra Logan took one look at the man across from her and *knew* it with utter certainty.

SIXTEEN

"Hey, how's 'bout lettin' one ol' timer buy another ol' timer a drink. Lookin' at ya, I don't see any room for an argument."

Marshall felt the first genuine smile of what seemed a lifetime crawl over his face.

"Scotch," Marshall said to the bartender, then turned to the man who had sidled up next to him, spilling over the trendy bamboo bar stool. "Thanks."

"My pleasure," said the man. "You're the first fella in this joint who is older than the scotch. 'Cept me, that is. Lenny Larkin."

"Marshall Logan," he replied, accepting the man's hand. Old money and new. Interesting. He'd shaken a lot of hands. It was amazing what a simple gesture could say about the man making it.

"Don't say?" Lenny challenged, a curious look splayed over the backdrop of sagging features. "I met a woman named Logan on the ship. Maybe you know her. Petra. Petra Logan. A fine little girl out here with some joker —"

"You saw Petra?" Marshall interrupted, blood pounding in his temples. "Where was she? Was she all right?"

"Slow down there now, Marshall. She was fine. Just fine. I take it you are acquainted with her. Not a jealous husband, I hope?"

"Worse," Marshall managed. "I'm her father. I'm here to find her. She's in some — well, there's something going on and I'm on my way to pull her out of it. Where did you last see here? She's supposed to be on Sava."

"I do believe she is," drawled the man. "That's where I last saw her. Left that boy of hers high and dry." Extraordinary southern emphasis on the *high* and the *dry*.

"Clark? She's with Clark?" Marshall thought the FBI had said she was in protective custody.

"Well, now I don't know about that," Lenny said, trying, between rattling gasps, to light the biggest cigar Marshall had ever seen, the flame of his gold-plated lighter disappearing into the brown paper for a few seconds before springing back to life. "He went back for her, but I can't say for sure he found her."

"You're way ahead of me, Lenny," Marshall said into a cloud of smoke. "How did they separate in the first place?"

"Had a little spat that last night. She said she wasn't going and Clark called her bluff." Lenny shook his head. "That Martin's not what you'd call the brightest crayon in the box. Halfway to Caracas and the kid gets a call from her. She's still on Sava."

A spat? Marshall's stomach lurched, the bits and pieces of the meal he'd picked at on the plane forming a hard, tight knot. Did Petra find out about Clark's handiwork at the bank? If so, she was in more trouble than she could possibly know, and knowing his daughter, she was handling it in typical form. That could be trouble. Big trouble.

"Do you know what the fight was about?" he asked anxiously.

"Couldn't help but hear some of it. The place we were stayin' at had walls as thin as a pauper's wallet. The disagreement was of a delicate nature. Being her father, you won't wanna hear the details, so let's just say that your daughter was not as enamored with the boy as he was with himself."

"I see," Marshall said. Relief flooded his tired bones. So Petra's objections to Clark were personal, not criminal. Well, she was safer that way, and he couldn't help but smile, she was also a little wiser about men than he'd given her credit for. Wiser than he'd been. But he'd gone back for her. Isn't that what Lenny said? Marshall didn't like the sound of that. She'd called him? Either she had escaped protective custody, or they were using her as bait. He'd didn't like the sound of either option. "You say Clark went back to Sava?"

"I had a hand in that," Lenny said. "He told me he had to get back to her. Patch things up. I didn't really want to; I thought your daughter was one hundred and ten percent better off without him, but he said it was what she wanted. That she'd called him. Well, you know your own daughter, Marshall." Lenny paused for affirmation, understanding. "I can't imagine you've turned her down on many occasions."

He was right. On the mark. Marshall had always tried to keep a stiff upper lip when it came to Petra and her craving for adventure but he had to admit more often than not, he'd given in. He could understand Lenny doing the same.

"You didn't talk to Petra, did you, when she called?"

"No, but my wife was on the deck when ol' Clarky boy got the call, said it cut him to his knees."

Something somebody should have done a long time ago, Marshall mused. Just leave it to Petra. Marshall could clearly picture the way her nostrils flared out when she got angry, the way her eyes turned a deeper, darker shade of blue.

There wasn't a whole lot Marshall could do now but wait. He didn't like this feeling, this total loss of control. This was something he had in common with his daughter and he hoped she was learning to deal with it as he was now. It would do her good. It might even save her life.

"Good evening, Mr. Ross," the bartender perked up several notches. "The usual?"

A man nodded wordlessly as he approached the bar and stood at the end of it. He was one of those men, Marshall noted, that needed few words. He filled up the space, emitted power and influence. The few females within striking distance sat up instinctively, the way their mothers had once taught them.

"What do you think?" Lenny asked in a loud whisper Marshall was sure the man heard. "Drugs or guns?"

"Could be both," Marshall answered, aware of the man's eyes upon him. He did not think his, or Lenny's presence, held his interest. Concerned him. He was taking in the room, observing his surroundings, his back to the only solid wall in the bar.

Lenny nodded, then ordered another round.

***

Had Frans known a more beautiful woman than Petra Logan and the way she looked at this moment, her eyes dark in the dim light, the shadows playing on her face?

She licked butter from her lips, her tongue pink, eliciting the very recent memory of its feel against his own. His shirt had slid down one of her shoulders, resting on the swell of her breast. He stared, mesmerized by the smoothness of her skin in the soft amber glow of the lantern. She caught the collar in her hand and slowly tugged it back up.

He followed the movement with his eyes up to her face. She'd been watching. Him. He saw in the depths

of her eyes, desire. Desire and something more. He
knew what it was because he felt it himself ...
something more. And then it was gone. She lowered
her eyes to her plate in a manner that struck him as
innocent, almost chaste.

Frans wondered about all those men listed in her
case file. Bullfighters to bowlers. Had the woman sitting across from him looked at them the way she'd just
looked at him? At Martin?

He smiled to himself as she tore off a piece of
bread from the loaf he'd put on the table, her eyes
lowered, avoiding his. No she hadn't. He also had
serious doubts that she'd even slept with any of them,
especially Martin, despite the assumptions her case file
made. Petra Logan might be fiery, but there was an
untouched innocence brewing beneath the surface of
that fire.

Maybe that's why she'd been so angry with him on
the beach – she'd been afraid – not angry. If she had
slept with other men, she hadn't been made love to.
Not the way she should be. It made him long to carry
her back to his lean-to and initiate her into the world
that was meant to exist between a man and a woman.

"What do you do, Petra Logan, when you're not
stranded on an island with a Burgomaster?" Frans
asked, needing to break their silence. Needing to think
about something else. Bedding a woman who knew
the ropes was one thing; seducing Petra Logan was
another matter altogether and not something to be
taken from her lightly, no matter how worldly she tried
to pretend she was.

She gave him a shy glance and then put down the
bread with a soft laugh, seeming relieved by the end
of the silence herself. "Not much, I'm sorry to say."

"Not much? What does that mean?"

"It means that when you've been raised in the lap
of luxury, there's very little that you are required to do

for yourself and no reason for doing it," she replied quietly.

"The world is a big place. There are many things to enjoy, with or without money."

Her smile was derisive. "Frans, all I've done all my life is enjoy myself. It loses its appeal after a while. I used to think there was a place for me. Something I needed and could do well, build a life around ..." She lowered her eyes again and poked at her food with her fork. Her words had been light, but her voice was apologetic.

"What about a family? Children? Doesn't every woman want a child?"

"You're sounding very European, Frans," she chided. "I've thought about children. In fact I adore them, but I'd kind of like a husband if I'm going to be a mother. To have one of those, well, I guess I'd like one who could see past my money, but it seems there's just too much of it for anyone to see beyond it. And then, I don't know ... what would they see?"

***

Petra pulled her eyes away from the Burgomaster and reached for her glass. Why was she telling him these things? Even her therapist didn't know this stuff. It wasn't the wine; she'd barely touched it. She took a sip. Maybe she should finish it. Maybe she wouldn't feel so exposed.

"I would think it's your beauty a man would have difficulty seeing past," Frans said to her as she raised the glass to her lips once more, his voice low in the quiet space between them. "But Petra Logan is nevertheless very visible and very charming. Many men, I think, would be proud to call her his wife."

The wine in Petra's throat formed a hard lump. The Burgomaster's steel-blue eyes pierced hers. No man had spoken to her this way. Ever. She swallowed. She noticed, however, that he hadn't said he was one of those men who would be proud ...

Suddenly, she felt the need to get away from him. Herself. Her emotions. The confusion.

"Where do I sleep?" she asked abruptly, placing her napkin on the table.

"On the bed," Frans answered without hesitation, rising and clearing their plates. "It's in back."

"Just the one bed?" Petra asked, trying to keep the mounting suspicion from her tone as she watched him cross to the cabin door.

He nodded. Smiled.

There had been only one bed back at headquarters.

Feeling suddenly feverish, she tried barring the images. His face next to hers, his lips on hers.

If they were only images, why was she blushing? If she was frigid (and she was, wasn't she?) why was she blushing at all? A whole year of Clark's constant pawing and nonstop libidinous suggestions (some she knew he either had to be making up or looking at the pictures upside down) hadn't produced so much as a warm thought. Yet, here she was, forced to spend the night with a man who'd practically held her hostage, was most likely lying to her about ... something and had the nerve to — to try and take advantage of her when she was obviously not capable of making sane judgements, and yet she felt as if the lantern's flame was racing up her body.

"So," she said, forcing each word out, "you'll be sleeping ..."

"I have not decided," he answered with raised eyebrows.

She wondered if her blush was visible in this subdued light. The cabin's space was so tight she could reach out and touch him, as if, no matter where he moved, he was always within her reach.

As if she was always within his.

"Would you like to go to bed?" he asked, pushing away from the dark wood wall. The flickering light made it seem as if she were moving towards him.

Did he mean ...?

They were adults. Candlelight. A romantic dinner. The gentle rock of the little, very private, boat in the moonlight. What else could he mean?

"I will see you in the morning," he said, reaching for the door, his wide back lashed with orange shadows. "Don't worry about the lantern, I'll get it later. There's a light switch just behind you."

"Frans!" His name slipped out before she could stop it. Where was he going to sleep? Was he leaving her by herself?

His huge shoulders turned slowly, barely, until his eyes caught hers. "Petra, is there something you want to ask me?"

Words stuck in her throat. Was there?

A smile crept over his wide mouth, and she felt the blood race to her head. "Is there something you would like me to do for you?"

She squared her shoulders. She'd already made a fool of herself once today; wasn't that enough? "I'll do just fine without you, Burgomaster," she answered cooly.

"Are you sure?" he asked, holding her eyes, his smile widening. "I think I've come in pretty handy so far. I'll be up on deck if you change your mind."

***

"I never liked Martin," Lenny said, the effects of his third bourbon sinking in. "Too slick for my taste. That girl of yours could do a whole lot betta."

"Amen," Marshall answered with renewed enthusiasm. It had been a while since he'd actually been to church but the sentiment was there.

"If ya don' mind my asking, Marshall," Lenny forged on without consent, "how, exactly, did the two of them hook up? I've been wondering since I met them. Petra's such a divine creature, well I don' have ta tell you, you're her father, and Martin, well, let's just say I've met my share of his kind in the six decades and change I've been around."

"He worked at my bank."

"Oh, I see. So, you know him pretty well."

"Thought I did, but I think he knew me better."

"Oh?" Lenny replied, leaving room for explanation.

Marshall sighed, the burden of worry heavy. "It's a long story ..."

SEVENTEEN

"No! Oh ... oh ... no. No-o-o-o!"

Frans bolted up out of the deck chair and stood motionless in the dark.

Petra! Had someone gotten to her? Flinging the cabin door open, he crossed the planked floor in two wide strides and thrust the long curtain back, his gun drawn as another piercing scream shattered the night in two.

"Augh ... stop ... no," she uttered frantically, her arms swiping at the empty space around her. Her eyes were half open.

She was only dreaming. Relief rushed through his body. She was alone. Safe.

Or was she?

"Petra," he said gently, reaching for her. As his fingers closed around her wrists, her struggle intensified, as she twisted and yanked to free herself.

"No! No, no, no!"

"Petra!" he said more forcefully. His hands moved to her shoulder and he shook her. Wherever she was, Petra Logan was in trouble. It was real to her.

It was real to him.

"Petra, wake up. You're safe. I have you now." He felt the battle within her winding down and pulled her into his arms. He stroked her silky hair. She was shivering.

"Oh, Frans," she sobbed, nuzzling her face, wet with tears, into his neck. "Oh, it ... it never goes away. Why won't it go away?"

"Was it the same dream?" he asked, drawing his head back, reaching for her chin. "The one about the lake?"

***

It had come again. In the night, the way it always did, but this time it was worse. This time the float hadn't been wrenched away. This time it had turned into an anchor and dragged her to the bottom of the lake. She tried to let go, tried to pull her hands free, but she couldn't.

"How do you know about the lake?" she asked when words returned.

"You said something about it, after your fall. You weren't really awake," Frans murmured into her hair. "I thought you were just rambling. Can you tell me about it?"

Could she? Other than the distorted versions that came to her at night, she couldn't remember a thing. "All I know," she sighed deeply into his chest, "is that I almost drowned in Lake Superior. A year ago. A storm came up, a bad one, and we were too far out."

"We? Who were you with?"

"I was with," she lifted her head, the name suddenly stuck in the back of her throat, "I was with Clark. He saved my life."

***

Clark Martin. He should have known. It all made sense now.

Petra wasn't in love with that greasy little scoundrel.

Her relationship with him had been based solely on gratitude, which he'd obviously twisted so savagely to his advantage that she'd probably agreed to marry him out of some sort of indebtedness.

Oh, to wring his scrawny neck for the way he'd manipulated this priceless, beautiful woman.

Not that he believed for even one second that the creep had actually saved her life. At least not intentionally. It was too much out of character. He'd been far too willing to hand her over to a hit man. Yet, Petra seemed convinced.

"How did he save you, Petra?" he asked, willing the disgust for Martin out his voice.

"I don't remember."

"Any of it?" How convenient for Martin, Frans thought. "Surely you remember something."

She looked away as if gathering her thoughts. "I remember the storm. When it came up. And —" Her face tightened, her shoulders bunched up. "I remember telling him ..."

"Clark?"

"Yes. I remember telling him that we had to go back, but it was too late. The water, it was in the boat, and I was looking for something. For a — a float. Something to hold onto."

"Did you find one?" Frans asked, watching her face intently.

"I ..."

"Did you find one, Petra? Did you find the float?"

"Yes, but," she bit her lip. "There was only one. I told him. Clark. I told him and ... that's all I remember. The mast hit me."

"Nothing else? Are you sure? Think, Petra."

"The only other thing I remember is waking up, on the beach," she said, suddenly. "Clark was there. He was ..." Frans felt her shudder and pulled a blanket up over her shoulders.

"He was what?" This ought to be good, Frans thought.

"He was ... saving my life. He told me."

Of course he was, Frans thought, brushing a wavy tress off her cheek.

***

She wanted to tell him more. Everything that happened that day and how it happened. Most of all, why it haunted her. Over and over. But she couldn't. She couldn't tell him what she didn't know. Remember.

She pulled the blanket closer to ward off a sudden chill. Almost instinctively, his arms tightened. But she had remembered something new this time. She was sure of it, but what? How could something so important keep slipping away from her? Right through her ... fingers?

No, not slipped ... pulled. Torn.

Ripped.

She closed her eyes, trying to remember.

Nothing.

She gave up trying and opened her eyes.

Vondel was smiling now. Not one of his big, boyish grins, but a tender, honest smile. "It will come," he said reassuringly. "In time."

He could be right.

What if it came tonight? As much as she needed to know, the thought of being pulled down again into darkness, real or imaginary, was more than she could bear.

"Know any good bedtime stories?" she asked, trying to lighten the mood.

"As a matter of fact," he said, with the return of the impish grim, "I do."

***

"Over there," Frans told her, pointing across the wide, watery expanse. He'd insisted they go out on deck, away from the chamber of her tortured dreams, so she could see the actual setting for his story. "It is where we were earlier."

Standing next to him at the bow, Petra followed his arm with her eyes to the slightest imprint of a bay in the distance. The water was still. Black. The thing he knew she still feared.

"The sandbar," she said, red tresses resting on her pale face. The wind picked up the loose hair and stirred it away from the smooth cheekbones before setting it back down.

"Yes," he said, slipping an arm around her. She didn't pull away, but he didn't draw her near. He just rested it gently on her small waist. "The sandbar. A very unusual sandbar. Mysterious, you might even say."

"Really, Burgomaster, mysterious?" she said, her voice catching slightly. Her response to his touch? Still her fear of the water ... fear of him?

"You have heard of the Sand Pirates, Miss Logan?"

"No," she said, shaking her head, curls springing loose from the makeshift shawl the flannel blanket had become. "I can't say I have. Perhaps, you could tell me about them."

"It's a tale not for the faint of heart," he cautioned in a tone he intended to be darkly teasing. "Pirates are a cruel, loathsome lot."

"Faint of heart? Me?" she said, tossing her head back, showering him with her laughter for the first time in hours. "Surely you jest, Burgomaster."

"Don't say I didn't warn you, Madam," Frans said pausing, his own voice catching. She rested against him, eased into his chest, unbidden. "Many, many

years ago, when Sava was an unknown land, inhabited
only by a small tribe of primitive —"

"Many years ago?" she asked with a small laugh, her
body stirring against his.

Frans gave her a stern look and resumed, trying to
ignore the fire she was lighting in him. "As I was
saying, the island, though not as big or as prosperous
as some in these waters, was revered by its people
because it was land. Risen up from the depths of the
clearest Carribean sea to provide its inhabitants a
home. A dry, safe place. Everything they had — food,
shelter — they owed to the land, the island, and they
were fiercely loyal to it. Their loyalty, however, did not
go unnoticed."

She let her head lean on his chest. Red feathery
wisps lifted to his face by the breeze, the pure sweet
scent of her intoxicating him. Did she know what she
was doing to him?

With effort, Frans continued. "As long as there
have been men, there have been pirates. Marauders
who take what they desire, loyalties to no one. No
place, no time.

The music and festivals of Sava attracted the
attention of pirates, and they crept upon the island one
night to learn what inspired such gaiety. Gold? Silver?
Precious stones? No, it was the sand itself the Savans
valued so highly.

The pirates decided they must have something as
precious as this to cause so much festivity."

She was staring out over the water, the moon
glistening over the bay, palm trees small and dark
against the night horizon. Was she with the Savans, the
dreams which haunted her forgotten in the yore?

"Many nights later," Frans went on, his voice
softened to a whisper, "while the Savans were sleeping
off a particularly eventful ceremony, two pirate ships
slipped into the bay. It was a quiet evening such as

this. They scooped up as much of the island as they could hold in their boats, and carried it away. No one was the wiser. Or, so they thought.

But the Island knew. The sand knew. It became heavy, heavier than the boats could hold. Until the ships began to sink. The pirates tried to throw their stolen Savan treasure overboard to lighten their load, but the sand would not forgive, and with every shovel they threw over, two more grew in its place until the ships overflowed with sand and sank to the bottom of the sea.

For years the wreckage of both ships lay there while the sand, in its rage, continued to flow out of them until a beautiful arch formed in the bay, burying the ships and its evil men forever. A sandbar. Low enough for small peaceful boats to pass over, but a bulwark against pirate ships. The sand, protecting a people who had honored it so greatly."

Frans nuzzled his cheek into her soft hair, no longer able to resist. "They say," he murmured, "if the wind is right, and the night still, you can see the pirates beyond the sandbar. Circling. Watching ... waiting ..."

"I can see them," she said softly, extending her arm towards the sea and the vessels sailing in for Sava's party. "See?"

"Aye," he answered, "pirates all right." One of them for certain. Involuntarily, his arms wrapped around her. A futile attempt to protect her from the storm yet to come.

Futile? Not if he could help it.

***

Petra liked his story.

She liked him. No, it was stronger than that. It was ...

She tried to remind herself that Frans Vondel was, among other things, her captor. Actually, as far as the captor bit went, on the whole, the experience hadn't been that bad so far — that is if you didn't count the two near-death incidents.

It was the *among other things* stuff that burned her up. The fact that he knew about her problem and seemed so single-mindedly intent on boosting his ego by curing her. She was surprised he hadn't asked her about it when he'd wormed the story of her nightmares out of her.

Oh, so that's why you won't let a man come near you! I knew it had to be something like that.

Yet here she was, fool that she was, leaning against his chest, wrapped in his arms, wrapped in the moment. The silence. And it was every bit as wonderful as she'd so often imagined it should be between a man and a woman.

How could it be so? She shivered. Clark had never made her feel this way. Never. Maybe it wasn't her after all, maybe it was Clark.

What kind of man is he? the Burgomaster had asked.

What kind of man was Clark Martin? Did she really know?

The Burgomaster had kidnaped her, kept secrets from her, had an endless stream of women passing through his door, and knew her most embarrassing secret, but — he'd saved her life, not once, but twice and had never been anything but kind, gentle, considerate, even affectionate at times. How was it that she felt she knew Frans Vondel better than Clark?

"Petra," Frans whispered, brushing the hair away from her neck with his lips. He was going to kiss her. She knew it.

He was going to kiss her until she couldn't breathe. He was going to kiss her and do all sorts of other unimaginable wonderful things and oh ... oh ... she was going to let him. She just knew it.

***

She lifted her face, opened her full waiting mouth to his kiss, and became his. He knew it. Petra Logan belonged to him. Completely.

The certainty of it filled him with a bewildering gratitude for having found what he had never known existed. A staggering love.

Lifting her, he gathered her into his arms, never wanting to release her again. Her arms circled him, hands in his hair. His mouth, with a will of its own, found her neck and she let her head fall back in invitation. Consent.

Her throat. Silky. Smooth. Her heartbeat racing beneath his lips. A warning sounding in his head as his kisses wandered freely — the timing was wrong. Dangerous. For her. And him. He had a job to do. He tried to clear his head, but was beyond reason.

"Ahem!"

EIGHTEEN

Petra wondered how she'd managed to hear the polite interruption above the wild hammering of her heart. Frans let her feet slip slowly to the deck. He was looking beyond her.

Petra turned to follow his vision.

The chicken man?

Minus his poultry.

He said something to Frans in that language they'd used before. Frans replied.

This wasn't a simple exchange of barter for her body. It was serious. Ominous. Their voices a deadly reverberation in the still night.

Frans's arm was holding her to him, but he was no longer aware of her. Not really. The chicken man had claimed his attention. Completely.

Clark Martin.

The chicken man had said it. She was sure. It wasn't her language; the syllables had lofted up and down, distorting it, but he'd said it just the same.

"What about Clark Martin?" Petra demanded.

Frans shifted uneasily beside her. His answer was a hard stare at the chicken man.

"What about Clark?" Petra repeated, moving out of his arms.

"Clark Martin? I can tell him about your former companion, but I do not think he will recognize him as a contender. Our friend here has come to make a much higher offer. He has a horse and two cows and promises marriage and does not accept my prior claim to you." He looked at her with his big Burgomaster grin, but his eyes were lying.

"He said Clark's name, Frans. I heard it and so did you. I could tell."

"Petra, words in another language often sound familiar. How would your new suitor know of your Mr. Martin?" Frans asked, his smile still teasing, but his eyes now utterly unreadable, void of lie or truth. Blank. Empty. This was a Burgomaster she had not seen before.

"You're lying to me, Frans," she stated simply, struggling to reign in the terror stirring within her.

Where was she? Who were these two men she was alone with on a boat in the small hours of the night? Strangers? Kidnappers? Murderers? What?

"Why would I lie to you, Petra?" Frans asked, his face softening with something else. Another unreadable expression.

"I don't know Vondel, why would you lie to me? Why would anyone on this island lie to me? I've been handcuffed, nearly murdered twice, kidnaped at least once, maybe twice, denied access to outside help and given none of the usual considerations a stranded tourist might be offered. Not to mention nearly seduced by the local Bluebeard."

She wanted to hit him. Beat him. Oh, what a fool she'd been. They were probably laughing about her all over the island. And that stupid pirate story. Who was the real pirate here? Probably the whole island was populated with nothing but brigands and thieves. "You've been lying to me from the start, haven't you, Vondel? What is this? An elaborate extortion scheme? What have you done with Clark? How do I even know he's on the Surf Queen? Is his body going to wash up somewhere? Oh, to think I almost threw myself at you!"

***

His fiery vixen had returned, but this was not the version he wanted. She was terrified. Of him. Did he leave her that way? Would she be safer, and more cooperative, calm or angry?

The whole operation was beginning to feel like one giant mistake. Rolphe was among the best in his profession. Frans had never before found reason to fault his work, but he'd made a fatal blunder saying Clark Martin's name. Frans himself was making errors in judgement, it seemed, ever since a certain redhead had come onto the scene, the biggest one likely being having prevented her from boarding the Surf Queen.

He looked into Petra's angry blue eyes. No, the biggest mistake had been falling in love with her. A blunder which could cost her life if he didn't sort this mess out quickly. He opted for calm. A willing captive was easier to keep around.

"Clark Martin has been involved in a serious crime, Petra," he said quietly.

"Clark? What kind of crime?" she asked, her tone derisive. "Pilfering tattered towels from that dump we stayed in?"

"It's curious you should mention laundry," Frans replied. "Mr. Martin has been pilfering, as you put it, from your father's bank by laundering money for an international crime ring." It was almost the truth. The laundering was, but it was Trumad he'd been stealing from.

"Clark?" Petra snorted. "As if! Clark might be many things, but he couldn't possibly have figured out how to set up an operation like that. That would take more brains than he has."

"I agree with you on that point, Miss Logan, but I can assure you he did do it just the same."

"You're lying!"

Frans gave her the last piece of information he was willing to give. Any more could pose risks to their entire operation.

"Do you not recall, Miss Logan, noticing a discrepancy yourself in a certain account, some weeks back?"

***

Clark, a money launderer? One of her father's most trusted employees? Her very recent former fiancé?

Vondel couldn't be lying about it. How else could he have known about that bank account she'd had investigated? She hadn't told anyone about it except Clark. Not even her father knew.

Investigated?

The realization of what she must have set in motion through that simple request nearly knocked the wind out of her. She gasped, groping for air.

"Petra," Frans said quietly, firmly, relentlessly. "This information must be kept to yourself. It is also necessary for your own safety that you remain in protective custody until Mr. Martin has been arrested."

Protective custody?

Petra looked into the eyes of the stranger she could have sworn she was falling in love with just moments ago. Protective custody? Is that what they called all the lying? What if she refused? She didn't recognize the hard, steel-blue eyes that locked into hers. But she did see there would be no refusing, no choice involved. She was his prisoner. She had been all along.

"You ... you!" There was no word. No description. "Who are you?" she demanded, launching into words she could say. "What are you? Why did you detain me?"

"Petra ..."

"Don't you call me Petra!" she seethed. "Don't you

dare! You call me Ms. Logan if you want to speak to me, you lying ... oh ..." The words were lost again. Then the revelation.

Bait. That's what she was.

They, whoever they were, Frans Vondel and company, were waiting for Clark to return to Sava to save her, so they could nab him, a wait the Burgomaster had spent wooing her to fill in the time. Keep her cooperative, so to speak. The swimming lesson, the kiss at Sea Front. It was all just killing time until Clark came back. Unbidden, tears fell, poured, from her eyes. Frans Vondel, if that was even his real name, had used her. Clark had used her. Everyone had used her.

"Petra," Frans repeated, soothing.

She couldn't speak, her rage was so intense. Blinded by tears, she pushed past him to the steps that lead down to the cabin. There was no place else to go. No place to hide.

***

"I think I blew it," Frans said in Dutch, leaning over the railing and staring unseeingly at the first hint of dawn stretching across the Savan horizon.

"Yeah, well you had help," Rolphe answered back. "I don't know how I screwed up like that."

Frans looked sideways at the man he'd spent more than half his career working alongside. They'd both made their share of mistakes, but this one was sloppy. Like the whole operation.

Deep down, none of his team had really thought they'd catch Trumad this time, and it was manifesting itself in a series of senseless errors. His own the worst of all.

Petra Logan. The variable they hadn't anticipated. She was supposed to have been a simple bystander they somehow managed to rescue before it was all over. A redheaded vixen who'd clouded his reasoning from the first words she'd spoken to him. Maybe even before then. Looking at it now, he wondered what had possessed him to grab her in the first place. Instinct? Or something else?

Petra. The spoilt rich girl. She was naive, sheltered, pampered and starving for love. She was a woman who required a special kind of care, not the indulgence her father showered upon her, not the fawning fortune hunters pawed her with, or the abuse that men like Clark Martin treated her to, but love. Simple love. Had she ever known the real thing? Had he?

Frans had his share of relationships over the years. His line of work brought many women into his life, but it also made permanence elusive, and looking at it now, Frans realized he had liked it that way. Companionship when he needed it, but few ties.

Petra would insist on ties. Could he give her that? He would want to. He knew that with a certainty, but staying with Interpol, would it be possible? Would he be happy if it weren't? He hadn't really known any other way of life.

Frans exhaled deeply into the humid morning rising over the bay. There wasn't much point wasting time contemplating it. She was justifiably deeply wounded, maybe too wounded to forgive him, but he had other things to worry about right now, like how to keep her alive.

Rolphe's confirmation earlier that the police station had been burned down was disturbing. His news now that Clark Marin had done it, if Eric's account could be trusted, and there was no reason it couldn't, only served to solidify Frans's suspicion that Clark had also been the culprit who'd pushed Petra off the pier.

Why Martin? He was hardly the standard hired-gun profile. Trumad was more meticulous than that. His hits were clean, tidy and untraceable. Quiet.

Frans clamped his hands together over the rail and bowed his head in thought. Someone was losing their edge here. Trumad? He doubted it. Frans Vondel? Possibly.

Clark Martin? Martin didn't have an edge to lose. That meant he was likely acting on his own. What would be his motivation? The question worried Frans. A lover spurned? An ego spurned? An ego resorting to murder for vindication? That had a ring of madness to it.

He raked his hands through his hair. A raving lunatic was exceedingly unpredictable.

NINETEEN

Clark had been squatting in the ditch for what seemed like hours. Waiting.

It was hours, the whole night, he realized, when he was no longer dozing in the dark. The sun was beginning its rise on yet another tortuous day on Gilligan's Island. Someone would come along now. Someone who didn't need their clothes as badly as he did.

***

"Lenny, Hon? That you?"

It would be him. Who else? Come to gawk at her in the tub. Examine the merchandise. Well, as dear old mama always said during those three-hour-long reinforcement calls that Lenny never minded splurging for, you don't trade a trailer for a penthouse without expecting a little something extra.

Mary Ellen sighed. That little something extra could take as long as an hour and she really wanted to catch that hunky actor in that new cop show. Dubbed, of course, but who cared? Suddenly she missed the trailer court. The boys had been a lot more fun and a hell of a lot younger than her husband.

Lenny clomped into the bathroom and Mary Ellen, in what could only be described as an involuntary action, submerged her new breasts under the bubbles. Quite a feat. Lenny'd sprung for the extra large ones.

"Change of plans, Baby Doll."

He grabbed a towel and held it over her. His face was red and puffy. He'd spent the night in the bar with that other old goat and then passed out when he finally made it up to their room.

"Lenny, I just put on this exfoliatin' cream and it takes —"

"No time. Gotta move, Darlin'."

"What are you talkin' about?" She was annoyed, to say the least, but softened, remembering mama's advice, "Sweet Cakes."

"We're goin' back to Sava but we gotta move fast. Boat leaves in —" He looked at his watch. He was serious. "Twenty minutes."

Sava? Why on earth would they be going back to Sava? They were in Caracas, for crying out loud. Who in their right mind would trade heaven for a rest stop?

"I ran into Petra's daddy last night and he's on his way to get her. She's in a bit of a bind over that Martin fella. Told him I'd go with. It's one of those man-to-man things, Honey, that I just don' have the time to explain now."

***

Petra? Petra's daddy? Mary Ellen tried to conjure up an image but, having never met her daddy, could not. Why would her daddy come? For her?

Clark?

It had to be Clark. What else? So, daddy wasn't welcoming Clark into the, stuck up (if she read Petra right) family with open arms. What a shame.

"Maybe I'm bein' a little selfish here," Lenny croaked, breaking through her thoughts, "thinkin' you'd be up for it. You could stay here. I'll come back when this is all said and done we'll have us a bang-up finish to this ol' honeymoon."

His choice of words.

Clark was a free man. Maybe he didn't know it yet, but if what Lenny was saying held water like a new tin cup —

"Course I'm up for it, Angel." She stood up and took the towel, inhibitions be damned. "Besides," she said, cupping his sagging cheek with her wet hand, "I couldn't let my sweet baby go off on his own like that. What kind of monster would I be? Poor little Petra. She'll need a shoulder to cry on. Be jus' a sec', Baby."

"Hot damn!" squealed her ancient husband with a luster she'd not experienced since they'd consummated their ridiculous, though mutually beneficial, union. "I don' deserve you, Mary Ellen Larkin."

Not by a long shot, she agreed.

***

The first car had not stopped. Or even slowed. He'd tried flagging it down quite gentlemanly, he thought, never even pointing the gun in the driver's direction, but the car had whizzed by with a gaped-mouth woman and several wide-eyed children.

At the faint sound of ... something, Clark readied himself for a slightly different approach.

Squatting in the ditch, next to the road, trying to be inconspicuous, his plan, if you could call it that, was to wait until the car was less that a hundred feet away, then pounce out into the road and aim. Aim to shoot.

He waited for what seemed like forever. Clark wasn't used to waiting, even under the best of circumstances, and a hot, smelly ditch on Sava wasn't one of them.

Something, someone, rounded the bend and Clark, agile and desperate beyond words, was ready. The fact that the oncoming vehicle was not motorized might have put off another man. He rushed towards her with all the pent up of passion of a man who'd been swatting gnats off his rear end most of the morning. She was fat. Huge. He almost felt sorry for the rubber tires that looked pressed flat against the dirt road. A Savan flag, clamped onto the bike's handlebars, snapped in the low speed breeze of her labored ascent. Lovely, he thought, straddling her path. Aiming the gun.

The basket on top of her head remained steady as if it were attached.

Basket?

Clothes?

"Eeee ... eeee!" she screeched. Clark took this as a distress call and widened his stance. That was a mistake. As she ascended on him, maneuvering the rusty bike like a circus performer, he realized what it really was: a battle cry.

"Eee ... yah!" she cried, swinging a massive calf into his chest, knocking him to his knees with one mighty blow.

Somewhat dazed, Clark scrambled to his feet, remembering the gun. She'd slowed the cringing bike to a wobble, craning her neck to gawk. It was easy to do now that the basket —

Strewn across the dusty road were its contents. Clark gathered them up while holding the gun on her. He didn't see any trousers but he'd go through them later.

"I'll count to ten," he said, not concerned in the least what language she spoke. It was tone. Always the tone. She peddled away with a less intimidating version of the battle cry, and he waded back into the safety of cover.

***

Frans stood at the top of the steps, arguing with

himself. Leave her stew or go down and try to talk to her. What would he say? That she was right? That he was sorry?

He'd used her. There was no way to soften it, even if he told her he loved her, and there was no reason for her to believe him anyway.

He drummed his fingers against the bulkhead a moment. He had to go. There was work to do. Rolphe would protect her.

Who was he kidding? Rolphe would guard her. Isn't that really what it was?

***

Mary Ellen thought they'd never get here.

The hotel was every bit as dingy as she remembered, and the stubby woman behind the counter, just as cranky. If she hadn't decided back in Caracas that Clark Martin, now available according to Lenny, was her true and only soul mate, she'd have stayed behind and waited for her husband in a hotel with tasteful rooms, friendly service and air conditioning. Love, Mary Ellen conceded, was made of sacrifice.

Petra's father immediately began grilling the woman about his daughter. He had a picture and showed it to her. Yes, she'd seen the woman, and yes she was doing fine the last she'd heard. She'd been staying at the station house out on the old road with the Burgomaster, but no one had been able to reach him since the fire.

"Fire? What fire? Was anyone hurt?" the old geezer demanded.

Mary Ellen didn't care about Petra or the fire, she just wanted to find Clark. If Petra was staying with the Burgomaster, whatever that was, where was Clark?

Marshall and the woman yakked until she thought

she would keel over. Petra this and Petra that. She was
sick of hearing about Petra. When Lenny and Marshall
finally decided to go out and try to track Petra down
themselves, she waived them on. Smiling. She'd do
some tracking down of her own.

With a big Southern smile, she turned to the
woman behind the counter. "Remember me?" she
asked sweetly. "I stayed here a few days ago? Mrs.
Larkin?"

The woman looked as if she'd never seen Mary
Ellen before in her life.

"We were with the other couple. The woman he
asked you about and her —"

"Yeah, yeah, yeah," the woman shook her head in
disgust. "Dat man, I don' like him."

I'm sure he'll be crushed, Mary Ellen thought, but
continued politely. "Do you know where he is? The
man that was with Miss Logan?"

"You got a husband?" the woman said sharply.

"I just need to talk to him." The woman's nosy
comment grated on her nerves, but she laid a twenty
down and asked again. "Do you know where Clark
Martin is?"

"No," said the woman, ignoring the money. "Don'
know and don' care. You do same."

"I'll do what I please, you old crone," Mary Ellen
mumbled under her breath, trudging up the worn
carpeted stairs. The woman was exasperating. Lenny
could be back any time, and she needed to be alone
with her future husband before she dumped her
present one. This was, for crying out loud, a very
delicate situation.

TWENTY

Frans stood in front of the mirror and gave the tie a final tug, the memory of swollen tears spilling over ruby lips dogging his thoughts like they'd been doing all day.

He forced his mind back to the tie in his fingers and the tuxedo Rolphe had brought to Sava a few weeks back. Fortunately, he'd kept it on the little boat they'd been using as a temporary base until the rest of the team arrived with technical equipment, costumes and props.

He hadn't been back to inspect the station house since the fire, but had heard, courtesy of Marta, that the place had been pretty much gutted. Most of his clothes would be ash. He grinned, remembering the box of clothes Petra had been so curious about, a hint of jealousy behind those incredible eyes. Eyes that had the power to make him question what the hell he was doing. Eyes that were likely still crying.

He cursed himself silently. Of all the stings and elaborate schemes he and his team had been through over the years, of all the roles he'd played, none had ever made him feel this guilt. There was no room for it in the job. And there was no room for it now.

He sighed heavily and scooped his keys off the night table.

"De party goin' ta be wild dis yere," Marta said when she saw him coming down the stairs.

She'd insisted on giving him a room in the hotel after she'd heard about the fire. Though he had no intention of sleeping in it, he'd obliged because he didn't want it common knowledge that he was staying on the boat. That Petra was on the boat.

"Eric be tellin' me a naked man try to steal his mama's bicycle dis mornin', right while she be ridin'!"

Frans laughed. "Did Eric's mama hurt the man?"

"No," Marta cackled, "He av a gun, but dat don' worry Eric's mama. She kick him, but he steal de washin'!"

Frans shook his head as he exited the hotel. A naked man with a gun. Hopefully, it was a simple matter of over indulgence on the part of a tourist and nothing more serious. The Burgomaster was going to be too busy tonight to deal with complaints of that nature. There were far more serious issues at hand.

He opened the door to the Datsun, his mind wandering with a will of its own to silken red curls and a pair of bright blue eyes. He surrendered his thoughts, giving up the fight. There was only one way he was going to get any work done tonight.

**

"How is she?" Petra heard Frans ask the chicken man, his heavy steps rocking the boat slightly as he boarded. At least they weren't speaking in whatever it was they'd been speaking before, Petra thought. Dutch?

There was no audible response. She assumed the chicken man had made some gesture. A shrug?

Then Frans said something in that other language. He was directly behind the closed curtain that separated her from her wardens. The chicken man left the boat. She could hear his footsteps climbing the small ladder leading from the dock up to the pier.

Petra backed away from the curtain. They were alone now. She and Vondel. And ... she was shaking. The curtain was drawn aside and he stood stooping under it, big and blond, wide-shouldered and muscled. Too big for the boat.

He had donned a tuxedo. For the party, she imagined. The party she'd only see from the porthole of her little floating prison. Not that she cared. A party for pirates and other sundry criminals and liars.

Frans Vondel, Burgomaster of Sava, aka whomever, was born to wear this tux. It was cut around him. His broad shoulders took control of it, filled it out. Showed it off. Tuxedos were the trademarks of her circle. Tight, shiny black suits with short coats and stiff white insets. Ingrained, initiated, as early as she could remember, she'd never grasped the magic.

Until now.

Petra bit her lip, her heart beating savagely. Why was she shaking? Why did Vondel garner such a strong physical reaction? Because her body was a traitor, she thought. When it finally responded to a man, it chose one that existed only in profile. Not real, just someone who took on whatever form suited the moment. A chamaeleon? That was too soft a description. Vondel was more lethal than that.

He was watching her intently, gaging her. Reading her. He glanced at the untouched trays of breakfast and lunch the chicken man had silently brought down and left on the table. "You should eat," he said.

She didn't answer.

"Petra," Frans said slowly, steel-blue eyes capturing hers, "I wish ... I ..."

The Burgomaster at a loss for words? That was rich. Was this his newest strategy?

"What do you wish, Vondel?" she asked sarcastically, feeling for the first time since setting foot on Sava, a small sense of control. "That I'd still fall into your arms, madly in love with you? Ignoring that you'd betrayed my trust on every level, that you'd used me, manipulated me, lied to me, tricked me?" She inhaled sharply to ward off lurking tears. "How long does the list go on? I'm sure there are still things I've missed. And for what? To catch a crook and satisfy your ego in the process? Surely I'm not worth that much?"

He said nothing, his eyes not releasing her, a thousand words in them. She tore her eyes away, turning to face the porthole, away from his power over her.

"Yes, Petra," came his hoarse reply, "I do wish that."

***

He wanted to tell her that he loved her, wipe away her hurt, say he was sorry, that he'd protect her with his own life, but there were no words to say it with, no words that would reach into her heart. There were no excuses. She'd been betrayed by him, Clark, everyone.

He touched her, needing her. She didn't turn, but she was in his arms, and he was kissing her, speaking with his heart.

***

She didn't look back, but his lips found hers. Without her consent, without her protest. She was drowning. Going completely under. He was everywhere. On her lips, in her mouth, in her hair, her shoulders ... consuming every inch of her ... every pore, every breath. Frans Vondel, or whoever this man was, owned her.

He couldn't. She couldn't let him. She barely existed as it was. She was just something men used for her money, her social position, or in this case, her place in the case. This man had used her worse than all of them put together. The others hadn't won her love and then destroyed her with it. She wouldn't let him take whatever she had left, whatever that was.

Petra pushed on his chest with the force of the rage she owed every man who'd ever wooed her.

***

It wasn't Chanel, Clark thought, as he strode determinedly towards the pier, but it was a dress, one of those long island things, large enough for two of him and covered with great gaudy tropical flowers on a red background. Not his best color, and he was trying not to think about the big yellow stain on the matching shawl and what it might be. He remembered himself, and pulled back his gait to something more feminine, keeping his eyes demurely cast down; wasn't that what a modest woman did?

"Oh, I don't believe this," Clark muttered, slapping away a grope with more force than was necessary, as he made his way down the splinter collection they called a pier. Another grope, followed by a wolf-whistle. These men were pigs. Savages. He clutched the tacky shawl more tightly over his mouth so his stubble wouldn't show. They wouldn't be so bold in the daylight when they could get a better glimpse of the beard he'd been sprouting.

As if things weren't bad enough.

Bad? Oh, things had gone way past bad.

Petra!

Clark vowed that when he found her, oh, and he would find her, she was going to wish she'd never met him.

I wish I never met you ... don't you ever come near me again!

All right, she'd already wished it but she wouldn't expect to see him, would she? Princess Petra was too busy throwing herself at that savage cop to even let it cross her mind. Well, well, wouldn't she be surprised? He couldn't wait to see her face.

"Ugh!" This was down right disgusting. Couldn't a woman walk the length of a pier these days without being assaulted? He gripped the gun, hidden in the folds of his ... ensemble. He had half a mind to —

"I wish I never met you ... don't you ever come near me again!"

"That does it," he told himself. This business of his voice yakking at him had gone too far. Now he was hearing other voices. Hers, to be specific. At full decibel.

"I mean it — whoever you really are, I don't ever want to see you again!"

That voice. Nails on a chalkboard. The voice that had haunted him for two days, that had yipped and yapped at him for a year. She was here. Somewhere. In one of the boats, putting off —

The cop!

Petra's cop. Coming out of a shoddy excuse for a boat. In a tux, no less. As if!

Clark had a tux. This year's Armani with the satin-trimmed boutonniere, a spectacular piece of apparel, left behind at that horrible hotel with that hag who'd likely sold it by now. And all because of, well, who else?

Petra! The ice princess who obviously hadn't melted after all. So it wasn't just him. It was all men. And to think he'd been wondering!

Clark backed up against the rail, and watched, waiting for the cop to disappear down the dock and into the crowd of party goers. The demon redhead was aboard that boat. He edged closer.

He couldn't see her, but she was there. Alone.

No, not quite alone. What was Petra doing now, hitching a ride off Sava in a leaky tub with another man? A local, and a wimpy-looking one at that.

Well, he might have to wait until he was sure that cop wasn't coming back, but Clark would have a nice surprise for her real soon. She could leave all right, but she'd have to swim.

Oh, silly him. Petra couldn't swim, could she?
Pity.

***

Perhaps he should regret having kissed her. He
didn't. Perhaps he should be worried. He wasn't.

Frans allowed a small smile to play about his face as
he strode along the pier, the Tuxedo feeling foreign as
it always did. He'd worn them often enough over the
years, usually in the line of duty, but he never could
feel at ease in one.

He let his smile broaden. Petra Logan was in love
with him. That kiss had told him so. She could deny it
and fight it, and scream and yell, but she couldn't
change it. He would get through this stint on Sava, and
then chase her around the globe if he had to.

"Toby!" Frans acknowledged, in simple greeting, to
a roughneck who nodded back at him with cautious
respect without pausing from his task of securing his
boat, the *Buccaneer's Princess*, to the dock.

The vessel was appropriately named, Frans mused.
The crew and their captain were nothing more than
modern-day pirates. He knew them by name, had been
on board, even shared a glass or two of whiskey with
them and ignored the contraband he'd noticed in their
cargo, as was expected of a simple island Burgomaster.
They had an easy, wary alliance: you don't bother us,
we won't bother you.

Outlaws of their ilk never concerned Frans; in fact
he liked to build a rapport with them. They were
dangerous and unpredictable, but they were also mere
stepping stones towards more formidable criminals
like Trumad and often as much use to the law as they
were the underworld.

Passing a kiosk, an island woman held up an

offering of curry wrapped in flatbread, but her grin
suggested she was willing to give him much more than
that. He declined with a teasing grin of his own,
moving onto the beach, surveying the crowds.
Catching Trumad was more necessary to Frans than
ever before; Petra made it more personal than before.

He'd never seen his own fallibility so clearly.
Operations of this magnitude were always unpredictable. Anything could go wrong and often did.

***

Standing on the upper deck, Alexander Trumad
studied the shoreline and the growing mass of revelers,
as his yacht, the American-registered Riva, pulled into
the busy little harbor of Sava.

Usually, he looked forward to this annual festival.
Sava wasn't good for much else, but they knew how to
throw a party. And it was one of the easiest places he'd
ever channeled money through. A perfect setup. He'd
been slipping in and out of Sava for years.

The locals were a quiet, stick-to-themselves lot,
who knew how to mind their own business.

"We're docking, Mr. Ross!" his crewman hollered
from below.

"At last," Trumad responded to his most popular
alias with comfortable ease and a flawless American
accent. Jordan Ross, American citizen no less. Plastics
mogul and playboy extrordinaire. He'd passed on his
usual cargo of buxom, brainless beauties to cart along
to the party. There'd be plenty to pick up off the
beach later.

For now, he had business matters to tend to, the
first of which was Martin. Miss Logan was a close
second.

***

"Whatta' ya spose happened here?" Lenny asked, hauling his ample, aging frame from the back seat of an ancient Toyota. "I mean, besides the obvious?"

Marshall looked over the smoldering remains of Sava's official police headquarters. "I don't know," he answered, "but I don't like it."

"Ditto."

"Got any ideas?" Marshall asked. They'd been puttering around the island for hours, in search of the one thing he was beginning to fear he'd never find.

"Well, actually, Marshall," Lenny said, steering him back towards the car, "I do. Driver!" he called into the wreck, "you know anything about this big ol' wingding?"

"Wing ... ding?" There was no hint of understanding in the jet black eyes.

"You know, son," Marshall pulled out a bill and tossed it on the front seat, "dance. Party."

"Party!" The young man nodded enthusiastically, burying the bill in his shirt pocket. "Sea Front. You go party?"

Lenny smiled and opened the door. "We go party."

TWENTY ONE

"Clark! Clark Martin!"

Mary Ellen looked high and low through the wild, crazy crowd but could not find Clark. She was running out of time. Lenny would get back to the hotel, find her missing and send out a search party.

She had the T-bills. The condo in Palm Springs was in her name and her checking account had about twenty grand in it. It wasn't much but Clark was on the fast track himself. He'd told her so. He was closing a deal worth millions but then Petra called and —

Petra.

What kind of woman was she anyway? Not the kind Clark needed at his side. She wouldn't even sleep with him. Everyone at the hotel could testify to that sordid tidbit. No, once Clark got a taste of what could be, once he got a look at her in this dress, Petra Logan would only be a distant memory. In fact, Mary Ellen would make that boy forget Petra ever existed.

"Clark!" she yelled into the party noise, hoping he would hear her. How many Clarks could there be at this party? "Clark!"

"You are looking for Clark Martin?" The voice was so close, so deep and perfectly clear that she nearly jumped out of her skin, which was almost as tight as her dress.

"Do you know him?" she asked, facing the tall, enigmatic stranger.

"Yes, very well. He is a friend of mine," the man answered. "I am expecting him to join me later on my yacht for an intimate party. Are you here alone? I would be honored if a woman as beautiful as yourself would keep me company until he arrives."

***

She was supposed to be a redhead.

She was supposed to be dead. A long time ago. At least it seemed like a lifetime ago.

He'd heard she was difficult. Alexander wrapped a smooth arm around her waist. If only acquiring Martin would be so easy. Obviously, handling Petra Logan was a problem specific only to lesser men. This was so easy, if she weren't so beautiful, he'd be bored. It wasn't even worth congratulating himself over. He smiled. Of course, the true test of a woman involved something entirely different. In private. Maybe he wouldn't dispose of her just yet.

***

There was music, loud thumping calypso and rhythmic reggae, tempered only by a noisy, boisterous crowd and the occasional blasting of fireworks which seemed to go off haphazardly, on someone's whim and in that easy-going island way rather than a set pattern.

The last thing on her mind was the party, but Petra was restless. She was hurt and angry too, and if she were honest with herself, still reeling from the Burgomaster's kiss, but twelve hours of being cooped up on the bunk had filtered down to simple boredom. How long did they expect her to sit in the cramped little room and, what, stare at the walls? Contemplate what a fool she'd been?

She was free to open the curtain and move about the galley, but not free to go up on deck. The Burgomaster had been clear and Rolphe, at least that's what the chicken man had said his name was after he'd started speaking to her in rather competent English, was on hand to make sure.

She'd peeked through the curtain a few times to see where he was, moving stealthily to it, scarcely breathing, and slipping it open so slowly and slightly that even she couldn't perceive the movement, but each time, Rolphe's beady black eyes greeted her unwaveringly from above the book he was supposedly immersed in.

Petra flung the curtain open. Since it was obvious there was no career in her future as a spy, she might as well go for the direct approach. "Are you in or what?"

Rolphe stared up at her, blinking his incomprehension.

"Poker, five-card draw," Petra said. "There's always a deck of cards somewhere on a boat."

"What are we playing for?" Rolphe asked, humorlessly.

"Fun."

"Fun?"

"Yeah, you know, fun," Petra said. She was bored, but she might also loosen him up, distract him maybe even. She owed herself at least at an attempt at an escape. Rolphe didn't look like the type to be distracted by beauty, besides like the rest of the island, he probably knew she was frigid, and well the Burgomaster had already staked a claim, hadn't he? Still, she had to try something. Something she was good at, like poker. Something she might be able to prick his male pride with. Only men knew how to play poker, right?

Well, she'd spent a month stint in Vegas while Troy, a Western League Bowling Championship Finalist, worked on his five-ten split. It hadn't worked out for them, it even seemed silly now, looking back on it, but she'd busied herself in the casinos while he'd practiced for hours and hours. She'd picked up a thing or two about cards.

"Sure," Rolphe said simply, "I'll look for the cards. You sit."

"Don't worry, Ralphy," Petra grinned sweetly, "I'll be as good as gold. I'm just bored to tears."

His response was a sullen shuffling through drawers and cupboards. He turned his head to tell her something as the cabin door burst open, hard, slamming the agent between the shoulder blades and knocking him down.

"Well, well, well," said a huge woman in a voice that sent chills up Petra's spine, "look who showed up at the party after all."

"Clark?" she gasped. In those clothes? With a gun? *Look who showed up at the party after all?*

He'd said it before. To her. She was sure of it. But when? In a dream?

"What are you —"

"I thought you might want to go out for a dip tonight," he said, fumbling with the shroud-like thing on his head, pulling it free. "And this time, do me a favor, would you? Wait until you're dead to wash up."

Rolphe lunged at Clark, knocking him to the floor and crashing on top of him. The two men grappled violently in the small galley, forcing Petra to crawl onto the table to get out of their way. She didn't like the way Clark's gun was waving madly about. She wasn't about to get in the way of a bullet. She hopped off the table and landed on the steps, realizing that freedom was just three steps above her.

Acting on sheer instinct, she clambered up them and into the night air, not stopping to look back as she hit the dock and climbed up to the pier, breaking into a run. She didn't know where to go, or what to do; she just ran. The festival was raging alongside her. Fireworks flashing, music and crowds a blur. She had to find somewhere to hide. Somewhere safe. Was there such a place on Sava?

***

"It's a zoo," Marshall complained as he and Lenny tried to penetrate the mass of whirling bodies. "We'll never find her in this. If she's even here."

"What?" Lenny yelled. "I can't hear a word."

"I said, we may never find Petra," Marshall bellowed into his ear. "But I think I just spotted your wife."

***

Frans circulated easily among the sea of people gathered at Sea Front for Sava's annual Barefoot Ball on the Beach. Tuxedos and sequins, sarongs and jeans, all mingling together, their common denominator, their bare feet. Even Frans.

Started over a hundred years ago by African slaves who danced on the beach, celebrating the only night of the spring they didn't have to work, the day before Ash Wednesday, it had just been a celebration for the locals. But some years back, one or two of the world's elite — bored and searching for new exclusive frontiers that middle class folk couldn't afford to get to — had decided Sava was the latest place to party; so they had come. In droves.

Half of them were likely criminals as notorious as Trumad, Frans speculated ironically, but Trumad was the one they wanted right now. They had enough evidence to bury him; they just didn't have him. His identity. His whereabouts. But he was close. Closer than ever. Frans could feel it.

His eyes drifted over faces in a seeming purposeless attitude. Just the simple Burgomaster, ensuring the festivities didn't get out of control.

It was his first Barefoot Ball. The locals smiled a

greeting, waved at him, or tried drawing him into a dance; he'd been the best Burgomaster they'd ever had, they all said.

The tourists, many of them having come to the ball for years, didn't know this new Burgomaster, but they didn't bother with him. Frans recognized a few faces from his travels. Cynthia Devries, middle-aged European heiress who usually graced the Mediterranean casinos, flirting with a disinterested Alain du Montagne, infamous Parisian nightclub owner and known drug lord, but active only in France. Jordan Ross, American playboy, who made his money in plastics, chatting amiably with Mary Ellen Larkin of all people. Frans smiled.

Amused, Frans watched them for a moment. Mrs. Larkin was way out of her league on this one, but she was probably already plotting her divorce from her hapless Lenny. Jordan Ross's tastes ran more along sleek, at least in public. Frans moved away from them and focussed on a more suited couple, fashion model Alexa Evert and the latest rock star she'd hooked up with. The scrawny fellow was quite likely using drugs, but didn't look like he had the brains to mastermind a ring the size of Trumad's.

He walked on, wondering what had brought Mary Ellen Larkin back to Sava. She had been on the Surf Queen with Petra and Clark Martin but it was docked in Barbados now.

Frans stopped and turned slowly back to look at her. Not at her. Her companion.

As if he'd felt Frans's eyes, Jordan Ross raised his head and stared at the Burgomaster. Trumad? Frans felt it. Saw it in his eyes, those windows to the soul, as the saying went. Jordan Ross and Alexander Trumad were one in the same. He was sure of it.

Frans rubbed the back of his neck, feeling the adrenalin in his veins. It wasn't the time. Not yet. He wasn't going to blow the whole operation over his instinct no matter how strong it was. If they didn't get him tonight, they'd get him later. Someone would either identify him, or he'd slip up, connecting himself to his true identity in some way. For now, for the moment, it was enough for Frans to know who he was.

***

Petra found a dark corner beside a stack of crates, and crouching behind them, caught her breath, blinking in an attempt to absorb the hustling activity going on around her, a sudden change from the austere quarters she'd been confined to since the wee hours of the morning. Men and women, all shapes and all sizes, wearing all kinds of things ... string bikinis, feathers and sequins. Tuxedos. One tuxedo in particular worried her. The one Frans Vondel was in.

She shivered, suddenly cold in the hot, sticky, Savan night. He'd done a fine job of protecting her, hadn't he? Three attempts on her life in as many days. At least he was consistent.

She had no doubts now, though, that the Burgomaster hadn't been lying to her about Clark being a money launderer. It was probably the only thing he'd told her that hadn't been a lie.

This time wait until you're dead to wash up?

Clark was referring to the boating accident on Lake Superior. Why had he said that?

Look who showed up at the party after all?

That's where she'd heard it before! Clark. On the beach. She remembered it now. All of it?

The float?

The float! And Clark, tearing if from her hands when she'd held it out to share, leaving her to drown in the lake. Clark, pretending he'd saved her.

The certainty of it, the memory, washed over her in

waves of nausea. He'd preyed upon her memory loss, twisting the truth and confusing her, telling her she was cold-hearted, even saying that was why all her previous relationships had been so brief, so fleeting.

The torturous year she'd endured! Small wonder his touch — he — had been so repulsive.

Oh! If he were here right now! What she wouldn't say to him! What she wouldn't do!

A large, stocky something in a dress, stomped along the pier in bare feet, searching. Well, okay, Petra reasoned, shrinking down even further, maybe she'd give him a piece of her mind later — when he didn't have a gun.

Clark passed on, and she allowed herself to breathe again. What had happened to Rolphe?

What now?

Vondel and his men would put her back in custody. Who knew how long they'd planned on keeping her hostage. Until someone succeeded in killing her, perhaps?

She assessed the scene in front of her. The pier. Busy and bustling. People everywhere and —

Boats.

Lots and lots of boats. Just like the crowd moving in and out of them, they differed immensely, but they all had one thing in common, she realized, weighing her options — they'd all sailed into the little harbor and, eventually, they'd all be sailing out.

Maybe, if she approached one of the ships and reasoned with its crew, she could be their stowaway. It was worth a try. What were her options?

Well, she thought, taking the first step onto her rickety road to freedom, this was it. Now or never. Do or die.

Petra heard the familiar sound of English. She stood up, her hair blocking her vision momentarily as the wind whipped it across her face like a flag, her red emblem, her father used to say, that he could pick out anywhere. She tucked her long mane into the back of the T-shirt Rolphe had given her earlier along with a pair of blue jeans that had come from somewhere. She didn't recall seeing them in the Burgomaster's infamous box of clothes.

Assuming a calm, casual demeanor was a stretch, but she managed it to some degree, and began evaluating the boats. A luxury cruiser, whose topless occupants were causing quite a stir with several males on the pier, was a pass. They'd probably welcome her, but ...

An even bigger, more luxurious cruiser was tied up on the other side, boasting several American flags. The Riva. Surely a fellow countryman would help her. She put a foot hesitantly on the wooden boarding plank.

How could she be sure the owner of this yacht would help her? What if he was a criminal? Hadn't Vondel said international crime ring? That wouldn't mean American then, would it?

She withdrew her foot. Nothing on Sava was as it seemed, and she had no way of knowing who she could and couldn't trust.

Farther along she noticed a scrubby, leaky-looking and roughed-up schooner bobbing in its moorings in that slow heavy way boats do. The *Buccaneer's Princess*. The crew was lolling around, some on board, some on the dock. Six of them. Huge and rough. Unshaven and dirty. Obvious criminals. The sort of men you didn't trust.

Obvious criminals who didn't hide what they were? Better the enemy you know than the one you don't?

They stopped when she approached, not that they'd been moving. It was more like they froze into a lethal silence. What should she say? Maybe she should tell them she was a fugitive from the law, a criminal too. She'd been driving a stolen car, hadn't she?

"Excuse me," she began, realizing as she said it,

how silly, how un-criminal-like it sounded.

A few eyebrows lifted, one or two pairs of eyes shared a glance, but no one replied.

Should she sound desperate? She was desperate. "Could you help me, please?"

Still no response, and Petra held back her panic when a particularly beefy rogue lifted his knife from its sheath at his waist and began to pick his teeth.

Oh! She just had to make herself sound bad ... nasty. "I escaped from the Burgomaster and ..."

That brought a response. Grins.

"What's so funny?" she demanded, annoyed. "Don't you think someone could escape from him?"

Outright laughter this time. Loud guffaws.

"I did. I stole a car." That was stretching the truth, but ... "He locked me up, and then another man came and tried to kill me and I got away. Now they're both after me. Please can't you just take me to another island? Now?"

Finally some interest. "How you pay?" a bald-headed fellow asked from inside the boat.

"I can't pay, I have no money, nothing."

"Petra!"

The unmistakable voice of her gun-toting, money-laundering ex-fiancé cut though the crowd like a knife.

"Oh, please! Please!" she begged, pointing to Clark. He'd lost the shawl but was trying to run in the dress. "If he doesn't get me, the Burgomaster will."

***

"Petra!"

Another glimpse of red. She'd tucked it into her shirt, but there was no mistaking her.

That boat. It looked familiar.

It couldn't be ... it wasn't possible! The men, that roaming brood of beasts who'd humiliated him and made him climb that awful ladder so they could rob him blind, and Petra Logan, daughter and only heir to MidWest State Banks, joining forces? Was there no level she wouldn't stoop to?

He hiked up his skirt and ran towards them, but the animals grabbed his fiancée and pulled her into their boat. He reached for his gun as they pulled away from the dock, then drew the gun back, more put out by the fact that they were now likely out of range than the knowledge that it would be stupid to cause a scene.

The hoodlums had the gall to wave.

If they thought he was going to stand for this, then they had just better think again. He'd already suffered their taunts and thievery but that, of course, was before. Before his fiancée decided to stay behind to sleep with the Burgomaster, before she'd jeopardized his business with Trumad. Before he'd had to hide in that scrubby Savan ditch just to steal the shirt, uh, dress on his back. Before he'd had to fight off that crazy man (another of his Petra's lovers, no doubt) and finally shoot him.

This time it was different. He had a gun. He had a plan. Well, an idea. All he needed now was a boat.

TWENTY TWO

"Bernard, forget de woman. It only make trouble. We got big trouble already."

Frans eyed the two large stooges moving clumsily through the throngs of gyrating people. Another gut instinct. Thugs, Petra had called them. The men from the white van, he was sure. And if that's who they were, then they were Trumad's henchmen. What lapse in judgement had possessed Trumad to hire them, or had he thought their unsuitability would be their best disguise?

He moved casually alongside them, screened by celebrants twisting in and out between them.

"She my woman, I marry her I tink," the shorter one insisted. "So strong, make many babies."

"She ugly, my cousin," his companion complained. "Like em dat way, hey Bernard?"

"She feisty. I know from de slap she give me. Too much woman for Alphonse, I tink?"

"I tink you make her to shave first."

Frans wasn't sure he wanted to know what they were talking about, but there was no accounting for taste, he supposed. He maneuvered himself a little further into the crowd. The pair was directly behind Jordan Ross, oblivious to him. They didn't know their boss's face.

Frans hung casually back anyway. Sometimes events had a way of turning in your favor for no apparent reason. His eyes wandered above the two goons' heads to Ross. He was strolling deeper into the crowd, chatting pleasantly to Mrs. Larkin who pawed his arm seductively and giggled something in his ear to which he responded with a modulated laugh

Bernard seemed to listen intently into the swarm of people for a moment and then exclaimed exultantly, "I hear him! Our boss!"

Frans felt his heart stop. Five years suddenly hinged on this short, stupid bandit. It was almost too easy. All they'd ever needed was someone to point Trumad out. And Bernard was going to do just that.

Before Alphonse could stop his cousin, he pushed through people, shoving them this way and that, as easily as if they were tall grass. "Boss!" he whispered loudly, following behind Jordan Ross, who, while continuing unfalteringly in his animated conversation with Mrs. Larkin, was also purposefully propelling her towards the end of the pier with increasing speed, which she seemed not to notice. She was going to be the new pawn in the game if they didn't do something fast. They couldn't let him get to his boat.

Frans spoke into the noisy air in short clipped Dutch, knowing the little instrument tucked inside his collar would transmit his orders.

"Boss ... Boss!" Bernard continued, still searching and Frans realized he still had no idea who he was looking for other than a voice. He smiled. Trumad should shut up.

***

"Boss!"

That voice!

Alexander Trumad cringed inwardly, continuing his conversation with Miss Logan, realizing by the blank look on her face that whatever he'd said couldn't have made sense. He picked up his pace again, but she didn't notice.

"Boss." Again. Then a shouted whisper just behind

his ear. "Boss! Meesaar Tru ...m-a-a-a-d."

Of all the glorious ways there were to go down, of all the scenarios he'd feared, this had not been one of them. Not that he was conceding defeat just yet. He'd come through closer calls than this. A dull-looking, meaty fellow grabbed hold of his arm. "Boss, I sorry. Alphonse sorry too!"

"Come again?" Trumad inquired politely, with the confused and controlled demeanor he'd perfected over the years. No one was going to trip him up. Ever. "May I help you?"

His arm was now being shaken violently, the whisper softer, but more direct. "Meessaar Trum-a-a-d. It us. Bernard and Alphonse. We sorry. We lose Martin. You no kill us?"

Later, Alexander seethed silently. Oh, to do it now, with his bare hands!

With a condescending smile, he let his eyes wander aimlessly around. The music didn't slow; the dancing remained frenzied, and the gaiety didn't falter. But there was a stillness screaming at him through a thousand pairs of eyes. Fixed on him? Moving closer? How could he discern anything with the bimbo attached to his other arm, babbling in his ear about who only knew what, vying for his attention. Where was that Burgomaster? If he wasn't around, this situation was manageable.

***

Above the chaotic sea of heads, their eyes met again. Locked. Spoke. The pursuer and the pursued. They were more intimate now than blood, reading each other's thoughts, knowing each other's next move.

Mrs. Larkin was the issue now.

She was dead. It was that simple. Trumad would kill

her purely for the vengeance whether they killed him or not, whether he got away or not; it didn't matter. A stand-off.

Frans's eyes never wavered from Trumad's. He could feel the team waiting for direction. He didn't dare move his lips. Signal. Not yet.

Bernard shook Trumad's arm once more and then stopped, his face paling as the nose of a pistol pressed into his ample gut. Placatingly, he backed away, bobbing his head in short little bows, Mrs. Larkin completely oblivious. Until now.

"A gun?" Mrs. Larkin screeched. "I know he was a pest, but that's overdoing it, don't ya think? You shoulda just told him to buzz off! I do it all the time."

Then Trumad made his fatal mistake. He took his eyes off Frans.

***

"Will you shut up!" Trumad growled out. No wonder Martin couldn't resist trying to kill her himself.

"Well excuse me for livin'! I suppose you're gonna point that thing at me now!" she babbled, utterly undisturbed by his menacing tone.

Trumad turned back to the Burgomaster, realizing too late, he'd made the most fatal mistake of his life. The signal would have been given. They'd be closing in.

He grabbed the bimbo's dyed yellow locks and yanked them with a force that made her scream as he put the gun between her eyes. "One more step and I'll blow Miss Logan's pretty little head right off!" He was going to blow it off anyway, but he might as well get as much mileage out of her as he could first.

"I'm not Petra Logan!" the blonde screamed hysterically.

The words startled him. For only a split second. "I don't care who you are you bimbo, shut up or I'll do you in right now!"

"I don't much care for the sound of that, son," a voice came out of nowhere.

Where? he thought, frantic for the first time in his life. Behind? Beside? How could he think with the broad screeching, "Lenny!"

Lenny? What in the hell was a Lenny?

When it knocked him to his feet, sat on his chest and cut of his air supply with a pair of eel-skin boots, Alexander Trumad figured it out.

***

"It's that fellow from the bar, Marshall. What do ya know about that? Didn't I say he was trouble?"

"You did," Marshall answered, impressed by Lenny's heroics and the sheer brute strength he'd mustered up to defend his wife.

"Oh! Lenny!" Mary Ellen cooed, diving into his arms once handcuffs were fastened around her attacker's wrists and Lenny finally took his foot off the man's windpipe. "You saved me."

Marshall couldn't help smile. There'd been more to Lenny Larkin than he'd thought; maybe the same was true of his wife.

It was amazing, Marshall thought, as he observed Lenny and his wife giving their statements, how hordes of lawmen had shown up like that, out of nowhere. Swarms of them. With radios and lots of guns. They sure didn't look like the kind of cops he'd expected to see on this island.

He'd been bang on, but the affirmation brought no consolation. It only intensified his worry.

How did he proceed now? Marshall wondered. He was here. They could hardly send him back. He approached one of the cops. The tallest one, the big blond one with the most air of authority.

"Sir," he said, interrupting a rapid exchange of

Dutch between the blond cop and a couple of other officers, "I'm looking for my daughter. I think she's here and that she's in some kind of trouble. Her name is Petra Logan."

The tall Dutchman gave him a long, evaluating stare, and Marshall knew he wouldn't get the truth. More Dutch.

A moment later one of the officers broke from their huddle and extended his hand politely. "Mr. Logan, would you be so kind as to come with me, please. I'm sure we can help you shortly."

Help him? My rear end they will! He was in for a load of malarkey, but what choice did he have except to sit back and listen to it? They outnumbered him fifty to one. And from what he'd just seen, they were probably doing a better job of protecting his Petra than he could ever hope to.

***

Feeling sorry for Marshall Logan, Frans turned his back on him and let the officer lead him away. They shared the same worry, but it wasn't time to set Petra free just yet. Martin was still running loose somewhere.

Frans raked his hands through his hair distractedly. Capturing Trumad wasn't the sweet victory Frans had always assumed it would be. He was glad. Relieved. But that was as deep as it seemed to go.

His sigh was heavy. His mind was with Petra and he sensed it always would be. The thrill of his job had been outshone by something much brighter.

What was Rolphe up to? he wondered, trying to put his focus where it belonged. Someone said he'd checked in awhile back, but no one had heard anything from him recently.

"Vondel!" An agent ran up to him with a cell phone. "It's Rolphe. He's been shot."

Frans took the phone, relieved that Rolphe was

healthy enough to be on the other end.

"I'm okay!" was the first thing out of his mouth. "Martin shot me in the leg, but when I fell, I hit something. I was out for only a few minutes, but the creep tied me up with a lady's scarf, then I couldn't find the phone and I couldn't walk."

Frans closed his eyes, waiting, dreading.

"Frans, she's not here. I think she got out while Martin and I were fighting."

***

Could it be? Clark mused.

Why, yes, it could. Not exactly what he'd hoped for but under the troubling, dire circumstances of this *exercise*, it would have to do.

Mutt and Jeff.

"Well, well, well, boys," Clark mumbled to no one in particular, moving swiftly (as swiftly as he could within the confines of the billowy skirt) towards the meaty mongrels, "time to put some purpose into your otherwise meaningless lives."

"Right about now," Clark added, coming up behind them and pressing his gun to Alphonse's head, "you should be hoping that if you don't have a boat, you at least know how to drive one."

Wordlessly the two looked at each other, at Clark, and then at each other, Alphonse's face naturally a little more worried than his cousin. "Trumad! Boss!" Alphonse babbled. "Boss! He —"

"Do you see your boss at this moment?" Clark demanded impatiently, to which they both replied with confused nods of *yes* and then hasty shakes of *no*. What had Trumad been thinking when he contracted these two? He was becoming more disillusioned with the organized crime king by the hour. Organized? That was a stretch. His first hint the guy wasn't all that he was cracked up to be should have been when he couldn't make up his mind where to meet — first it was Sava, then Barbados. No, then Sava again. He was worse than a woman. "Who has a gun to your head? Me or Trumad? In case you can't figure it out, I'll tell you. It's me. I have a gun pointed at your head, so that makes me the boss. Right?"

***

Frans pushed down the panic pumping through his blood. He had no time for it. Right now he had to think fast and clear. Where was she?

She'd be hiding around the pier somewhere. He was sure of it. Maybe she'd be moving around the yachts, trying to stowaway or convince someone to give her a ride off Sava. He'd find her. He had to, before Martin did.

"She go wid Kendrick and Toby," Eric said, trotting beside him on the pier, keeping up to Frans's gait with effort.

Good old Eric, Frans smiled. Every town around the world had an Eric. The urchin nobody bothered much with, who saw everything, knew everything, missed nothing.

He patted the boy's head which was bobbing subconsciously to the reggae beat that had started playing again. Frans doubted even a revolution would stop the Barefoot Ball. "Where did they go, Eric?"

"Look like maybe Eden Island. Toby always go dere."

"Thanks Eric," Frans said, "I owe you, boy. Maybe someday you'll be Burgomaster."

The boy's eyes shone at the compliment as he headed back to the beach.

"Frans, de man who stole mama's dress. He steal boat. He go to Eden Island too," Eric called back. "Maybe I be better Burgomaster than Frans!"

"Maybe so, Eric!"

Maybe so, Frans repeated mentally, waving over a boat, the fastest one in the harbor. His people.

TWENTY THREE

"Oh, yes, I did meet her," Petra was saying, sitting comfortably on the quilt Toby had so thoughtfully stretched over the wooden bench, "but no, I've never met Madonna."

She hadn't won over all of the crew just yet, but she was working on it. Kendrick, the surly, baldheaded captain, still seemed to think, having learned how wealthy she was, having so foolishly told him so herself, that she'd bring in quite a ransom and a few of the other rogues looked at her like they had other more unmentionable ideas in mind about what they ought to do with her.

Toby on the other hand appeared to be quite smitten, and being as he was the largest of the bunch, Petra decided she, for the moment, was reasonably safe.

She had no idea where they were taking her, nor did she care. Away from Sava was good enough.

***

Frans was gaining on the *Buccaneer's Princess*, his boat being faster and about forty years younger. He'd passed Martin and Trumad's thugs several minutes back, not bothering with them, other than to radio back their location. Clark Martin was nothing compared to the danger Petra was in with her band of pirates. Their treatment of her could shift with the wind. And would. Moreover, there were hundreds of small islands peppered throughout the Caribbean; if he lost her now, he might never find her.

He had insisted that all backup follow at a healthy distance. If he was going to pull Petra out of the clutches of Kendrik and Toby, he had to be alone. They'd kill her without blinking if he came any other way. He was banking on his relationship with them to work in his favor.

***

"Can't you make this tub go any faster?" Clark bellowed, jamming the gun into Alphonse's head. He didn't know why he kept doing it; it did nothing to increase their speed, but it did make him feel better. They could have stolen any boat in the harbor, but no, Bernard and Alphonse knew somebody. Had friends.

And that cop! That stupid cop had passed right by them as if they were of no consequence. Well, he'd soon think differently.

***

"Dat rat!" Toby exclaimed, passing the binoculars to Petra.

Vondel. Gaining on them. Fast.

"Can't you shoot him or something?" Petra asked, not really meaning it, but hoping they'd do something to evade him. They were all criminals, weren't they?

"No, very bad ting to shoot Burgomaster," Toby said. "Makes much trouble. De Burgomaster is good to Kendrick and Toby. He no see tings."

"He doesn't see things? You mean like, what, drugs?"

"No, no drugs. Tings."

Frans's boat pulled up alongside the *Buccaneer's Princess*.

Petra expected the crew to hide her or something, but they didn't. They simply slowed to an idle and stared at him. It was the same scenario they'd put her through on the pier. The old earn-our-respect routine. Good grief! Why did it always have to come down to something macho between men?

"Kendrik!" Frans called up, cutting his engine. "You have something I want."

"Maybe I be wantin' it more!" Kendrik called back, coming to stand by the railing.

"Let's trade."

"Trade?" Petra screeched. "I'm not a piece of property to barter over." She grabbed Kendrik by the arm. "I do as I choose."

Kendrik briefly turned to her. It was an instant so quick, she might have missed it were it not for the sheer menace of it.

"Fine, fine!" she said, backing up, "Barter away!"

"What you give me?" Kendrik demanded.

"Remember that incident three weeks back? The stabbing in the bar? The man will live, he's not so hurt. I'll forget about it, okay?"

Kendrik appeared to consider this, then called down, "Why she wort' so much? Maybe I keep her anyway."

"I love her, Kendrik! I want to marry her!"

"What?" Petra shrieked in disbelief, leaning over the railing and almost falling overboard, except that Toby caught her.

***

"There they are!" Clark cried exultantly, his boat finally catching up to the cop and Petra. "Pull up beside them," he commanded Alphonse.

"I love you, Petra," the cop was yelling.

"I remind you that she is my fiancée!" Clark yelled back, but no one heeded him. Not the slugs on Petra's boat, nor the cop. Why was everyone ignoring him? Seething at this extreme insult, he pulled out his gun and fired. Someone would pay attention to him now!

"Abana' sheep!"

Albino sheep? Clark turned around to see what the crazy fools, Bernard and Alphonse were talking about now. Maybe he should shoot them too. They were beyond annoying.

Perched on both sides of the outboard motor, tipping the little boat nearly on end so Clark had to hang onto his seat, the two fleshy bookends jumped into the water.

Odd, he thought. Even for them.

Clark dismissed them as the front of the little boat bobbed, nearly flopping over. When he looked up, in the hopes of spotting his faithless and all-too-*lucky* fiancée, he was met with a nauseating, surprise.

Guns.

Huge guns. Monster guns. Many guns. All pointed at him.

Albino sheep? No, no, no ...

Abandon ship!

The water was colder than he'd expected. He freed himself from the heavy fabric of his dress and paddled away from the boat. The pirates. The cop. Away from *Petra!*

***

"Oh, no! Frans!" Petra screamed, jumping into the ocean, Toby following behind her. Several more splashes.

The water around Frans was spreading with blood. She tried to hold him up and was swallowed by men. Talking. Yelling above her. Lifting him from her. He was limp, conscious, but barely.

Someone lifted her out of the water and placed her

beside him, placed his head in her lap. She touched the wound on his chest, wanting to stem the flow of blood.

"Ouch." His half-closed eyes met hers and she nearly lost it. But she couldn't.

His face went still. Lifeless. And yet, there was life left in him. She could feel the blood pumping against her fingers. She could feel every beat of his heart and ... every beat of her own.

TWENTY FOUR

A thousand hours.

She couldn't wait another second to see him and yet, if she had to, she could wait a thousand days. For this man. This *love*. His. Hers.

She'd named it, claimed it, knew she couldn't live without it the moment she'd nearly lost it, forever. In the water, her foe no longer because this love was stronger.

Theirs. It made her want to weep.

She was weeping. She'd been weeping for hours. Weeping. Waiting.

"Miss Logan?"

Petra's head jerked up, her eyes meeting those of a woman dressed in hospital garb and holding a chart. A doctor?

She sprang out of her chair, her heart beating so fiercely she could feel it in her ears. Let him be all right, she prayed. Anything. She'd do *anything*, just let him be all right.

"Mr. Vondel is in recovery. His injury was not as serious as we'd first thought."

Recovery? Frans was in recovery?

The doctor was still talking.

"He's going to live?" she interrupted, needing an absolute.

The doctor assessed Petra with a sweeping look. "Not if he keeps jumping in front of bullets."

***

He'd got the cop. That was something.

Clark clutched the float and wondered what time the sharks fed. He'd ditched the dress finally, watching it sink out of sight with more pleasure than he'd have guessed.

They'd ignored him of course, in their panic to get that cop medical attention, but it had been the one time in his life Clark had been happy for the lack of attention.

Bernard and Alphonse, those wimps, had begged for mercy and been pulled in. Not Clark Martin. That would be the day he begged for mercy from anyone! A boat would happen along. He was convinced of it. He even had his story ready. He'd been in one boating accident already; borrowing graphic details from it should make his story quite entertaining.

A boat rose up on the horizon. Well, he hadn't had to wait long, had he? He began waving. Did he look frantic enough? He waved harder and added a few yells.

It was a yacht. A big yacht.

A woman leaned over the side as it pulled near and called out. "Hey! Sweet Cheeks, what are you doing out there all alone?"

Clark looked up to the deep, intoxicating female voice. "I'm, ah, taking a dip. Care to join me?"

"You are a naughty boy," the woman said, bending over the water so Clark could get a good look at her. Not bad. A little ... sturdier than his tastes usually ran but ...

"I see," she said, taking in his body with a slow, lingering gaze, "you forgot your bathing suit."

"I didn't forget it," Clark said, offering one of his better smiles.

"You really are a bad little boy aren't you? Why, I have half a mind get you on my boat and teach you a thing or two."

Clark smiled. He still had it. Oh, yes he did. He had it and she wanted it. Bad.

"Here," she said, tossing a rope ladder out to him.

He climbed it with agility, finding a small place for gratitude to those pirates for having initiated him.

She pulled him up with an unusually firm grip and strength. "Well, I must say," she said as he emerged in his entirety, "what you lack in clothing you make up for in ... personality."

Oh, yeah, Clark thought, feeling better than he had in days, she wanted him.

***

Marshall Logan watched the way they moved together, coming down the pier towards him. Natural, he thought. As if they'd been together for years, but with the excitement and playfulness of the first stages of love. For the first time in her life, his daughter seemed to be truly happy. Deeply happy. Glowing, but grounded.

"I love my daughter," he'd told Vondel, "more than anything else on this earth."

"I know the feeling," he'd answered, looking Marshall full in the eyes.

They were going to stay on Sava for a while, maybe longer. Vondel was going to continue on as Burgomaster until the Dutch government found a suitable replacement, but it didn't look to Marshall like either one of them was in any hurry to leave the island. It'd be a long flight to visit the grandkids ... maybe he'd bring Joan with him.

As they neared Frans's arm slipped away from her shoulders and lingered, familiarly, on her back. "It's been an honor meeting you, Marshall. I hope we see you soon."

Vondel had a strong, confident handshake.

"You can count on it," Marshall answered, looking one last time into face of the man he was entrusting his daughter to. A good face, he thought. Solid and honest.

"Oh, Daddy," Petra said, wrapping her arms around his neck, holding him tight, the way she used to when she was a little girl. He felt the wetness of her tears against his neck.

"Call me once in a while, will you?" he muttered, his throat catching.

"Every day," she promised.

                         ***

"So, Frans, you never did tell me what happened to Clark."

Frans smiled down at her, amazed that this beautiful woman had deigned to give him her love.

"He was picked up, I suppose you could say."

"Arrested?"

"Eventually."

"By whom? How?"

"By one of our operatives, who, shall we say, really doesn't mind which way his gate swings open."

"Oh," she said, not comprehending at all.

They strolled along the pier, pausing for one final wave at her father as the *Surf Queen* started out to sea.

"Now, about that box of clothes?" Petra asked with a raised hand to block the kiss he was about to bestow.

"Madam, surely you know that in a place like Sava, with its roots in piracy, information of any kind does not come without a price," Frans replied, kissing her hand instead, seeing as she wouldn't let him have her lips.

"Okay, Vondel, let's cut to the chase. How much does information like that set a girl back on Sava?"

Frans grinned. Marta had brought over that box. A

collection of castoffs tourists had left behind over the years, but he didn't see why Petra needed to know that for a long, long, time.

EPILOGUE

Petra rolled over and was pulled back into a massive chest. She let her hand run over it, relishing its hard warmth and smiled. Frigid? Her? Hardly. That's what Frans had said when he finally got around to asking why she'd been so mad at him on the beach that night. He was right, she concluded with a blush when she thought about all the long nights since and the things they ... she ...

"You weren't thinking of escaping, were you?" His morning voice was husky, his breath warm on her cheek.

"Escaping? From the formidable Savan Burgomaster?"

"Yes," he answered, his hand working its way up her back. "Unless, of course, Madam, there is another Burgomaster after you."

His fingers were in her hair. Soft and tender.

"I think one Burgomaster will do."

"And husbands?" he teased, kissing her neck.

"One Burgomaster, one husband," she said circling his neck with arms, pulling herself up so her face met his. "I'm set. For a while anyway."

He smiled. Always that smile. "Madam, do you know the penalty on Sava for trifling with a husband's affections?"

"Oh," Petra said, looking into his sleepy grey eyes and biting back a smile, "would you believe I forgot? Again? Do you think you could ... show me?"

"If you insist," he said, bringing his mouth to hers.

ABOUT THE AUTHOR

ELLIS HOFF has lived in and around Minneapolis all her life and resides now in the small town of Medina, just west of the city with her husband, daughters and son. Bitten by the writing bug in the fourth grade, she's thrilled to see her words come to life in her first novel, Sand Pirates. She enjoys reading just about anything, as long as there's someone falling in love, and has a soft spot for biking, camping and the ever-changing seasons of the northern Midwest. Ellis abandoned the idea of relocating to a warmer climate about the time she decided to quit the daily grind and take a stab at making writing more than a hobby. The long, cold winters are perfect for inviting in the *heat* of a good romance.

Don't miss out on the latest news from Ponder Romance!

"Ponderings"

Ponder Romance's biannual newsletter, featuring the newest Ponder Romance, the latest of delightful escapades by the very romantic, Dominick Miserandino, and much more! Complete the reader survey below and we'll put you on our newsletter mailing list!

Please circle the appropriate answer/fill in blanks:

1. Was this the first Ponder Romance you've read? *yes/no*
2. Which novel did you read?.....................
3. On a scale of 1-5, *(1 poor, 5 excellent)* how would you rate the novel you read? ....
4. Was there anything in particular you did not enjoy?.................
....
5. Was there anything you especially liked?.....................
....
6. What is your opinion of the cover?.....................
7. How often do you read romance novels? *regularly, occasionally, rarely*
8. Would you read another Ponder Romance? *yes/no*
9. Where did you obtain this Ponder Romance?.....................
10. Your age: *under 18, 18-25, 26-34, 35-50, over 50*

_____

Name

_____

Address

_____

City   State/Prov.   Country

_____

Code

Mail to:

Ponder Publishing Inc.   Ponder Publishing Inc.
PO Box 23037, RPO McGillivray   60 East 42nd Street, Suite 1166
Winnipeg, MB R3T 5S3   New York, NY 101655
Canada   USA